The
AWAKENING
OF
MAGIC

BOOK ONE
of the

WEREDING
CHRONICLES

Christian Boustead

DISCLAIMER

This work contains violence and nudity so be warned.
No person living or dead is described in this book and all events are of a
fictional nature.

Published by Christian Boustead
Publishing partner: Paragon Publishing, Rothersthorpe
First published 2015
© Christian Boustead 2015

ISBN 978-1-78222-383-2

Book design, layout and production management by Into Print
www.intoprint.net
+44 (0)1604 832149

To my family, who believed.

ACKNOWLEDGEMENTS

I would like to thank the following people:

My brother Adam, who has had to put up with me and my writing for years; my parents John and Pauline; my other brother Daniel, and the rest of the family. I must also thank Anne and Mark at Paragon Publishing for all their help with this book.

If I have forgotten anyone, then I apologise.

CONTENTS

PROLOGUE

"The darkness only makes the dawn more beautiful."
Takana the Harpy from the Wereding Chronicles by the Red Wizard.

Eloo opened her emerald eyes to see oak leaves rustling above her, their broad rounded shapes silhouetted against the grey light of dawn. She wondered what had awakened her, and realised the body she expected to be next to her was gone. She twisted round in the soft pelts forming her bed and looked towards the inner chambers of her tree house, but even her faintly glowing green cat eyes could not see any trace of the one she sought.

"Kye?" she whispered in her deep and sultry purr of a voice.

She got to her feet with the wild grace of an animal, and stepped out of the bed and down from the raised platform to stand in a crouched position that would allow her to jump in any direction if it became necessary. Her long mobile, cat like ears pricked for a response to her call, but none came. She could hear nothing except the rustle of leaves and the occasional snap of one of the hangings serving as walls in her open plan tree house.

Eloo drew the sharp air of dawn into her large nostrils. Her powerful sense of smell detected the familiar scent of leather and strong musk. The perfume of her lover, but it was old and fading as she sampled the air. She sniffed at the nearest hanging, but the cloth only smelt of dew wet wool.

Closing her eyes, she turned her sight inwards. Calling up her elemental nature she drew upon the mystical power running through her veins, its source her very spirit. Eloo enjoyed this part of power summoning, as the focusing of energy warmed her blood as if a furnace inside her had been turned on and was building force.

She found the mild heat the summoning generated made her light headed. It was a buzz which could be addictive, but Eloo knew what would happen if she pushed her powers too much. Still, she enjoyed the feeling of euphoria as the power built inside her.

When Eloo felt the necessary energy had collected she sent it outwards, her thoughts going with it. As she did this she turned in a circle. Though not aware of it consciously, as she spun her ears flicked forwards as though listening to the magic.

Her powers allowed her to sense the mind of a living creature within the reach of her magical senses. Still, she could not find Kye, but neither could she detect the thoughts of any hostile intruder. However, she did detect a flicker of thought just on the edge of her sense's range. It was too distant for her powers to be able to scan the mind and move at the same time. She would have to get closer to the flicker to detect its intentions – hostile, or otherwise.

As she passed through the hangings of her bedroom, her hand plucked a small leather satchel from where it hung on one of the shaped branches serving as doorways. She slung this over her left shoulder. Padding soundlessly across the wooden flooring, she drew from its sheath around her neck a long, slender dagger. The dagger, her Athame, was more a focus for her magic than a weapon, but its slight weight in her hand always made her feel better.

As she moved, she ran through her mind the magic at her disposal. She wished she knew some defensive magic, but they were the province of the Schools of Earth and she was a being of air. Being a witch, she was not denied access to such spells and could cast them. However, she never felt comfortable with them and they never worked that well for her. If she cast an earth spell it would either be only half as effective as it should be, could fail entirely, or cause strange effects that could be dangerous to her and anyone else in the area.

Her teeth gleamed in the dark as she reflected that the best form of defence was offence. Reaching into the pouch, she retrieved a small drawstring bag which held some light powder, and clutching it ready she glided forwards towards the unknown mind. She paused just before the rungs of the rope ladder leading to the forest floor, and gathering her powers again sent out her senses, but to her relief she recognised the mind now. The mind was sleepy, but its surface thoughts were as clear as her own.

"Need drink."

Going to the edge of the tree house's platform, Eloo looked down to see curled at the foot of the oak a large, grey wolf, its head only just rising from where it had lain on its paws.

"Fang."

Its ears pricked and rolling onto its back it looked up at her. The wolf, seeing who it was, happily thumped its tail on the forest floor, sending up several fallen leaves which flashed like water drops thrown up by a splash. Eloo grinned back, for the wolf's delight was infectious.

"Where Kye?"

She did not speak in the wolf tongue, for although she knew a little of the language and had spells allowing her to communicate with Fang, Kye had trained the wolf well enough that he understood simple commands.

The wolf looked up at her and then back at the ground, his nose close to the leaf mould. This was, as Eloo knew, his way of saying, "No I don't know but I can find out."

"Find Kye."

The grey huffed in response and began to trot off in the direction Eloo already suspected Kye to have gone. However, to find out where the wolf would lead her she had to get down to the ground. Stepping to the edge of the tree house, she gathered her energies again and activated another manifestation of her air nature. Jumping out into mid-air she summoned a wind strong enough to counter her fall, so she floated to earth as if she were a feather.

Landing in a crouch she sprang to her feet and following the smoke grey shadow, slipped like a ghost through the tall oaks and ashes of her home forest.

Eloo found Fang sitting at the edge of a large, perfectly round pool. Sitting beside the wolf, his dark blue eyes mirroring the pool, was her lover, Kye. Eloo, standing under the trees edging the clearing, studied his back. His tall, lean form appeared pale in the dim light of pre-dawn, but even in this light her eyes could make out his shoulder long black hair she loved to run her fingers through. She could tell from the tilt of his head that he stared into the water and was probably not aware of the smoke skinned wolf beside him, let alone her presence. Here, however, she was mistaken. For as she considered his pale and naked form, he spoke in that soft, if hoarse whisper of his.

"What are you looking at, Panther?"

"The eyes in the back of your head, Moon man. How long have you been up?" she asked, as she padded up beside him and looked down at the mirror still lake.

"Since moon set."

"Something troubles you?"

"You know how I love the new moon," was his offhand reply.

"The Lady has died, yes. But you know as well as I, she will be born again."

"It's not just that," he said, his broad shoulders shrugging her comment away. "There is something coming, some kind of change."

Eloo crouched down beside him and reaching out, ran a finger down Kye's back. Her digit traced the line of grey hair outlining his spine.

"Have you had a vision?"

He growled, shuddering with pleasure at her touch. "No. As you say, the Silver Lady is at her weakest."

"Then what?"

"I don't know," Kye said, shrugging. "It's just a feeling."

"Just a feeling?"

"Not exactly. I smell it in the air, I hear it in the wolves cries, I feel it in my bones."

"You're sure it's not part of the change?"

"No, the wolf within is an old friend," Kye said with a wolfish grin, revealing long canines. "No, this feels like a sending, but I can see nothing in the waters."

Eloo, hearing his words, looked down at the pool before her, but all she could see was the glittering jewel of the last star, reflected from the dark mirror. Then the rim of the sun rose over the canopy of the forest and a glint of red touched the water. As it did, a scream tore through the stillness of the dawn.

THE POISONED BLADE

"No poison bites like a Werewolf's blood."
From the Book of the Wolf.

For a long time nothing moved or spoke, even the birds that greeted the sun with their welcoming voices were silenced by that cry of pain and rage.

Then Eloo asked in a hoarse whisper, "What was that?"

"A woman's cry," snarled Kye, leaping to his feet. "Fang, scout."

The wolf, leaping to its feet, shot off into the trees like a grey streak of smoke.

"It came from the stone arch," Eloo said, her head cocked to one side as she listened.

"Here!"

Kye tossed Eloo a cloak with which to cover her slender nakedness, himself pulling on a pair of woollen leggings.

Eloo wrapped the cloak about her and belted a sword over it, while Kye pulled on a thigh-length tunic and slung a quiver over his shoulder.

"Can you reach Fang?" Eloo asked, as they began to move through the woods.

Kye paused, and closing his eyes used his innate magic to look through Fang's eyes. Out of Kye's throat there clawed an animalistic snarl and when his eyes snapped open they were no longer blue, but a feral yellow.

"It's Kain!"

"Here!"

"Hurry, he's attacking someone," growled Kye and he rushed off into the trees.

When Eloo arrived at the small hill which thrust its bare head above the trees, she found Kye had been right. The tall, lean figure dressed in black could be no other than Kain, only he went around in the wolf helm. This figure's head was clad in a large full head helmet crafted in the likeness of a snarling wolf. This figure was indeed fighting with someone else, a young woman from the long

11

red hair flying about her as she danced back and forth.

Eloo wondered where Kye could be, when a black feathered arrow flew out of the trees to her right. The bird of death, meant for the wolf helmed figure, was knocked aside by some small winged thing. Even as Eloo realised what it was, the glittering object flew at her like some wild bird or large insect. But, as she knew, it was an edged bird and it was only her cat-like reflexes that saved her from being cut.

Her blade sprang like a living thing from her sheath, to fly up into the glinting bird's path. A clash of metal and Eloo had to dance back and make a figure eight with her sword to fight off the thing.

Her enemy became visible to her in the morning light. It was as she had suspected; the little thing was a flying dagger. The blade's cross guard, a pair of large, glittering wings, beat into blurs as they tried to propel the blade past her guard. Then Fang leapt out of the bushes and grabbed the blade's hilt between his pearly teeth. The wings beat furiously, but Eloo scooped up a handful of the sandy soil and poured it over them. The earth countered the air magic enchanting the blade and the wings went still as the knife literally went into shock.

Acting before the blade could recover, she plucked it from Fang and embedded it into the ground and with a quick, strong twist broke it at the hilt. The wings, which had begun to flutter, went rigid and Eloo gasped as she heard in her mind the scream, as a demon, or spirit, was released from the cursed weapon.

Meanwhile, the red haired woman who had until now been keeping her attacker at bay with a long sword, cried out and fell to one knee. The wolfman who could be Kain yelled in triumph as he withdrew his long sword's blade from his opponent's shoulder. The wolf attacker raised his weapon to strike, when Kye charged out of the trees on his left, an arrow in each hand. His eyes gleamed yellow and his lips peeled back from fang like teeth. His long, black hair streamed out behind him like a dark comet.

The wolf helmeted figure heard his snarling challenge and spun to meet him. As Kye charged up the gentle slope towards his opponent the dark mailed figure began to chant. His claw tipped fingers made weird twisting motions, and his blade drew symbols in the air. Seeing this, Eloo, who knew a dark magic when she saw and heard it, hissed like a cat. Drawing herself to her full height (of just under five feet), and gathering her strength and magic, she called up her anger and hatred and her fear for her lover, and with a cry she unleashed her magic at the figure, calling the name of Lightning as she did.

From behind closed lids she saw a flash of almost blinding light, and when she looked up from where the force of her summoning had pushed her, she saw the black armoured figure face down on the ground. His cloak was burning and his body jerking from the electric bolt Eloo had unleashed upon him. But Eloo also saw Kye had been stopped in his tracks. A globe of black, web like strands had engulfed her lover and she could see Kye struggling to cut his way out of the net.

Eloo wanted to take advantage of this attack, but such a burst of magic had momentarily drained her energies. Drawing on her elemental essence she pulled air deep into her lungs, feeling energy flow into her veins. Feeling bolstered, she gathered herself for battle.

"Time to end this," Eloo hissed, and strode purposefully towards the twitching figure.

But as she marched up the hill, the figure sprang to its feet, discarding its cloak and spinning towards the two uprights topped by a capstone that marked this hill. With a word of the ancient tongue, the assassin flung a handful of dark powder into the arch. As Eloo watched, an inky darkness formed between the stones and she realised she was looking through the arch into a room beyond.

"No!" she screamed. Without thinking she hurled her sword at the retreating figure. But Eloo was too late and the figure passed through the stone door. The flung blade struck an invisible barrier that had sprung up behind it once it had passed through the gate and as Eloo rushed forwards the darkness disappeared and she could once more see the trees, framed by the dark grey of the unfeeling stones.

Eloo retrieved her blade and to her relief it was undamaged. She turned her attention to the red haired figure who lay on her side, a hand clamped to the gash in her shoulder. As Eloo bent over the body, she saw it was indeed a woman. A young and very pretty one at that, though her features were now contorted with pain.

"Get away!"

This girl might have tried to attack Eloo, but Kye's foot had come down on her blade, pinning it to the ground.

"We mean you no harm," Eloo breathed, trying to take the girl's hand away from the wound.

"So you can enchant me," the girl spat.

"We just saved your life, girl."

Kye had ignored all this and dabbed a finger in the girl's blood. He gingerly licked the finger and his face twisted into a snarl of disgust. "Black bile! The hell hound has poisoned his blade."

The girl moaned and passed out.

"Can you neutralise it?"

Kye glanced at Eloo and then at the west. She did not have to scan his mind to know what he was thinking.

"It's a new moon, I know, but can you try anyway?"

"If you can try to heal her."

"I will try, but most of my healing potions are back at the tree house. I would go get some, but I am not sure she would last long enough for them to help. I might have an acorn in my satchel."

"Let us try, then."

Eloo watched Kye turn to the west where the moon had set an hour earlier, attempting to implore his goddess to give him the power to neutralise the poison. Unfortunately for the girl, the new moon was the time (apart from eclipses), when Kye's goddess was at her weakest and therefore, by extension, so too, Kye. That was to say, his magic was at its lowest. Still, as she watched his bowed head, she heard his low voice chanting, attempting to invoke his powers. She was not sure that even if he wanted to Kye could be a conduit for his Silver Lady's power, still that was his concern.

Hers was to attempt to heal the damage done by the blade. She opened the leather satchel at her side, and plunging in a hand, found to her relief a handful of acorns. Now how to get the girl to eat them?

Eloo tried to wake the girl enough to have her swallow, but she only moaned and turned away from Eloo and towards Kye's chanting.

Eloo gritted her teeth and decided she would have to try a spell of her own. She might be able to pass the healing magic, which she had imbued into the acorns, onto the girl via sympathetic means. If she ate an acorn, would she be able to pass its magic to the girl? She had never heard of such a thing, but magic could be strange.

Eloo needed to draw again on her internal power, but she had taxed her resources, so she reached out to an external force to help her. Closing her eyes, she reached out with her mind, feeling for the Sylphs, the powerful air elementals which were, at least in essence, her sisters. "Sisters I appeal to you, give me your strength, so I may help another."

Eloo did not receive a response in words, but she did receive an influx of strength as she drew in deep breaths of the empowering air. She felt power flow into her and she muttered her thanks to the Sylphs as she prepared to begin her casting.

Taking a candle from her satchel she made a shallow dish like impression in the ground and set the candle into it. She lit it with a magical word and removing a small slip of parchment from the satchel, she first inscribed the inked letters to memory and then held the parchment to the flame, reciting the spell as it blackened and curled to ash.

"I call upon the Lady's healing light to purify this child before me. In the name of the Goddess I pray this wound will go away. So may it be!"

As she said this, she closed her eyes and opening herself called upon the Goddess to help her. Almost at once, she found a strong source of power. The stone arches had been held as a temple for hundreds of years, so Eloo fortunately had a source of power upon which to draw. She imagined herself a tree with its roots deep in the ground, but which had its head in the clouds. She drew on the magic radiating through the air and focused on the girl lying before her, attempting to channel this energy through her Athame and into the girl's body. She felt a wave of power pass through her.

Abruptly the power vanished, and she was no tree or conduit, but just a woman of flesh and blood and a weak one at that. She opened her eyes, but the world spun around her, as the blackness of exhaustion pulled at her senses.

She might have fallen as she swooned, but Kye's strong arms embraced her and held her up. She looked into his dark blue eyes and saw concern written there.

"Are you all right?" he rumbled at her, a look of concern glittering in his normally veiled eyes.

"Yes, I'm fine, if a little spent. Did we succeed?"

"You did. I have only managed to slow the poison for a few hours. Long enough I think to obtain a cure from the groves."

"Then the Lady is not completely dead?"

"No, but she is sleeping. I meant to neutralise the venom, not delay its effects."

"What about her wounds?"

"As I said, you succeeded. The wound is closed and looks as though it is at least a day old. I don't know what magic you found, but it is powerful."

"Too powerful," Eloo sighed, feeling another wave of weakness sweep over her. "I think I may have drunk too deeply from this well. I feel so drained."

"The Triple Goddess is strong in you, my love."

This made Eloo smile, but grimly. "That she may be, but if so I wish she would treat my body a little more gently. As you know, Kye, I, too, am weakened at this time by the Silver Lady's death."

He did not say what he was thinking, but Eloo, who could read him like a book, did not need him to break his taciturn silence to know he was asking himself how she did it.

"Then how was I able to work such magic? You forget, Kye, this place is a temple to the Goddess and has much power stored in its stones."

A raised eyebrow from Kye spoke a thousand words to Eloo, who knew how to listen to his face and body, and knew what he was asking.

"How can I use the stones when I am of the Air?"

He nodded.

"Because, my dear man, the power may be stored in the stones, but it is, after all, a place of air and air elementals live around it. The energies living in the stone radiate through the air and the water lying beneath it, and so I can draw on magic even if I cannot access the stones themselves."

Fang had, by this point, loped up to his friend and looking up at Kye he barked at him.

"She is fine, Fang," Kye said, his dark eyes never leaving Eloo's lithe form.

"Though in need of meat and drink and a long rest. Kye, could you fetch me some food or one of my draughts from the tree house?"

He lowered her to the ground, but before he left her he stooped, and rising with his lithe grace, offered the acorns she had dropped in her haste to heal the girl.

"The girl is healed, but you could do with the cure."

She smiled a thin, tired grin and taking them popped one into her mouth and began to grind the hard nut. As she did, she felt the warm glow of the healing magic seep into her blood and though she still felt a little light headed, she did not pass out. However, she needed to regain her strength. Still she had a welcome source of power available to her, for she lay in the early morning sun and like some great cat, stretched out to bask in its warming rays.

"Oh, Horned God, your kiss is very good today."

When Kye returned a moment later with a flask of berry wine and some smoked rabbit, hastily plucked from one of his many bolt holes, she was almost asleep and watched him from under her heavy lids. She yawned, and stretching, sat up, propping herself up with one arm in a half sitting position.

Kye, measuring her fatigue, knelt beside her and with one hand proffered the food and with the other arm supported her back.

"What would I do without you?"

Kye did not respond to this question, but left Eloo and moved to the girl, to further their healing work by binding a poultice of his woodcraft around the wound. The bandage would keep out infection while helping to heal.

"How is she?"

"Asleep. I think she may be out for the next day or so."

"Better that way. She doesn't seem to like us."

Kye did not reply, but returning to where Eloo was sitting he took from her a scrap of meat and tore off a strip. After chewing and swallowing, he tossed the remaining bone and its morsel of flesh to where Fang sat, slobbering, a few feet off.

"She has no doubt been taught to hate us, like most of the humans."

"Well, let us hope we can change her mind."

Kye grunted, and throwing back his shaggy head, took a long pull from the wine flask.

"Where shall we put her?" Eloo asked.

"The hammock."

Eloo smiled and nodded her agreement. "What about the antidote?"

"I'll send a message to one of the Silver Shield and have them bring a Hale berry out here. It should be here by nightfall. She should last that long."

THE WOLF, THE CAT AND THE ROSE

"Those of us who have magic flowing through our veins, wear our natures on our sleeves. If we wear any that is."
Takana the Harpy, from the Wereding chronicles by the Red Wizard.

Rose swam up out of the black sea of unconsciousness, to find herself surrounded by green. She was, she realised, looking up into leaves and she was moving, as though rocking in a boat. She tried to move, only to find herself bound in a bag or robe.

She raised her head painfully and looked along the length of her body to find herself not in a boat, but tied into a hammock of some kind and a blanket swathed her body, fastened securely with a strap. At first, she thought it was to stop her from going anywhere, but as she struggled she found she could get her arms out with a lot of effort and she realised the aim of the binding was to stop her from falling out of the hammock.

Turning on her side she found she hung beside a wooden platform. As she realised this, she became aware of two other things. The first being that somewhere, something smelt very good and it made her stomach growl like a waking dragon. The other was the low chanting coming from somewhere beyond the brilliantly coloured drape hiding the platform's interior. Where was she, how had she gotten here? Then, like a tidal wave, the memories came flooding back to claim her in a wave of black horror and despair.

"Father!" Rose moaned, remembering the last few hours of her life. She remembered the flashing steel of her father's blade, contrasting with the attacker's black sword. She remembered her father in his white robe, and the wolfman in his black mail. She remembered the blood, flying up like a red fountain. Then the world swam around her, as a veil of tears came between her and the leaf filled sky.

Eventually she got her grief under enough control to wonder how she had gotten here and why her shoulder burnt with a cold fire. She tried looking, but couldn't quite see so she felt and found a bandage of some kind binding her shoulder.

She also realised she was wearing no top. She had been wearing her dark green dress, but she felt like she wore nothing but her pants.

She tried to get out of the hammock, but it began to sway and made her dizzy. As she did a shadow fell across her and she looked up to see a figure standing nearby. The figure of a man, from what she could make out, though for some reason she could not see him clearly.

"Don't move yet, you're not strong enough," came a deep, if gruff voice which sounded hoarse, as though the owner did not speak much.

"Where am I?"

"In the northern woods of Mercia."

Rose shuddered, as she asked the question she was dreading to know, "In the Wereding Woods?"

"If that is what you call them," came the reply. "Don't move."

She was going to ask why, when the hammock she was in began to move. She gasped in surprise as the hammock first jerked upwards towards the tree canopy and then swayed towards the tree house. It was only as she felt it bump against a hard wooden platform did she realise she had been swung in so she was no longer hanging above air, but was now in the tree house. She had only just taken this in when with startling suddenness the figure appeared above her. She gasped, and instinctively drew back from it.

This would not be surprising, for was getting the first glimpse of him. She saw a tall man, dressed in earth coloured tunic and leggings and this was not remarkable, but what was so startling was his face. Rose had never in all her life seen such an animal face, long and lean with the almost underslung jaw of a wolf, and blue eyes gleaming yellowish in flashes of light. His hair was long and black, but touched with silver (not grey but silver) at the temples, and his jaw was covered in long grey hairs. When he gave her a grim smile he displayed the long teeth of a predator.

Rose knew (though she could not have said how she knew for she had never seen one), she was looking at a werewolf. Never in her life had she seen one whose face mirrored the animal within.

"Sit up." Though his voice was gruff, an underlying gentleness had crept in at seeing her reaction.

Rose did so slowly, aware of the removed binding and the slipping sheet and what this would reveal. The wolfman appeared not to notice that under the sheet she had bare and well developed breasts.

Instead, he handed her a wooden bowl of some steaming soup. She looked down into it, wondering what was in it. She had heard many stories about werewolves.

"What's in it?"

"Rabbit," was the harsh reply and looking up into those eyes she saw them change from blue to yellow and back to a dark, almost black blue.

Rose took the bowl and raised the wooden spoon to her mouth. It certainly smelt good and not until she tasted the first delicious mouthful did she realise just how hungry she was.

"It's delicious, thank you."

The wolfman grunted and turning, shouted to someone beyond the hangings. "Eloo, our guest is awake, finally."

Rose heard the singing stop and a second later the curtain was swept aside to reveal a figure almost as startling as the wolfman.

However, where the wolfman was scary, this figure was beautiful, in the way in which a tiger is beautiful. She, too, had long black hair, but whereas the man's hair was dark, this woman's hair was the darkest black Rose had ever seen. Looking at it she felt as if you could be lost in it. The hair was swept back and fell to her waist, pulled behind her long cat like ears which were pointed and which moved as if they had a life of their own, as did a short prehensile tail.

The cat woman looked at her with a pair of green eyes, which glowed slightly in the dim shadows of the canopy. This cat woman was so short she barely came up to the wolfman's elbow, but she filled the space she took up with a whirlwind presence and when she grinned at Rose, Rose couldn't help but smile back.

Though the girl did display her own set of fangs, there were other things about her. The first thing Rose noticed was the reason why the wolfman had not bothered about her nudity. This girl was all but naked and despite, or perhaps because of, her size she sported a pair of breasts which made Rose's sizable mounds look small in comparison. Rose blushed at this observation, and the fact that the girl was wearing only a belt and a knife or something round her neck only made it worse.

The wolfman, who was leaning against the tree's considerable trunk, must have been watching her more closely than she realised, because his next words, though they were meant kindly, made her blush darker.

"My dear Panther, I know you prefer to feel the air against your skin, but our guest is not used to it and you are embarrassing her."

"Oh, am I?" the cat woman asked, in a deep voice which purred like the cat for which she was named. "In that case perhaps she should get out of that hammock and then she would be as dressed up as much as I am."

Rose blushed and pulled the sheet closer about her. The wolfman grunted and disappeared behind the drapes. He returned with a cloak of brown cloth, which he held out to the woman.

"Very well, if you insist, my dear Kye."

Kye, if that was his name, did not reply, but simply held out the cloak, which with a deep, if theatrical sigh, the cat woman took and fastened about her though it emphasised, rather than hid the size and curves of her femininity.

"I had a green dress?"

"Did you?" the cat woman replied, as if she had no idea whether Rose did or not. "Kye, did she have a green dress?"

Kye did not reply in words, but vanished again to reappear with her dress and, more to her relief, her father's sword, in a sheath of leather.

"So you did," the girl said, grinning in an expression of pure delight which was hard to resist.

Rose was surprised by this woman. For although her father had always told her the elves were not the monsters her nurse made out, she had heard so many stories about how the elves (and that was surely what this woman was, though she did not look like Rose expected her to look), were dark sorcerers and would enchant you and enslave you to their wills at the first opportunity. Was this what this woman was doing to her? She was charming, but Rose did not feel her mind was being ensnared.

"Who are you?"

"Oh, please forgive my manners," the woman purred, dropping a curtsey. "I am Eloo, and this is my lover, Kye."

Rose looked at the werewolf and he nodded, as if to confirm he was indeed Kye and he, too, greeted her. Rose realised he was like one of her father's household guards, the strong silent type, who did not waste time on words and would give you a grunt rather than a flowery speech.

"And you are?"

"Before I tell you that can you answer a question?"

"If I can."

"You are what I think you are. You're Weredings aren't you?"

A snarl clawed its way out of Kye, but it was followed by Eloo's laughter.

"Weredings, fey, fairy that is we. If you haven't guessed already I am an elf and Kye is a werewolf, but he doesn't bite unless you ask him to."

Rose looked in the werewolf's direction, to find his blue eyes looking straight back at her. Now, however, he was silent and his face might have been carved from stone, so motionless was it.

Eloo spoke again, jerking Rose's eyes back to her.

"Your name?"

"I am Rose Can…" Rose stopped, realising her family name may not be one that was welcome in these lands.

The girl seemed not to notice her hesitation, though Rose was not sure if she had noticed it and just brushed over it or if she had not noticed, but she was sure Kye's dark blue eyes missed nothing. She thought he had given a slight flicker of reaction at her name, but it was impossible to be sure. His face was a mask and his dark eyes were hooded, though they did glint yellow at times.

"So how do you know Kain?"

"Kain?" Rose asked, thrown by this question. This woman's thoughts were darting in all kinds of directions and she could not keep up with them.

"The man you were fighting."

"I don't know him. I have never seen him before today."

"It is not today you met him. It is twelve days since you came to us," Eloo broke in.

"Twelve days!" Rose said, taken aback by this revelation. How could she have been asleep for so long?

"Kain poisoned his blade with a particularly nasty venom. You were lucky Kye and I were able to heal you when we did. However, it took longer than we expected for you to recover."

"I had no idea."

"Kain," Kye broke in, steering the conversation back in the direction he wanted.

"As I said, I have never seen him before. I and my sister, Robin, were going to pick some berries when we found our father fighting this monster. We were frozen for a moment and as our father told us to get to the house he was... he was..." Rose broke off, unable to bring herself to actually say what she knew to be true, this Kain had struck her father down.

"So you grabbed up the sword and followed Kain through a gate to here?" Kye's voice was emotionless, but it made Rose look up in amazement nonetheless.

"You speak it as if you were there."

Kye grunted and shrugged, so it was left to Eloo to explain.

"Kye has deductive powers, he has simply reasoned back from how we found you."

Rose started, recalling something she had forgotten.

"Robin! She will be wondering what has happened to me!"

"I have family in the cities, I will ask them to search out your sister and let her know what has happened to you."

"Thank you!"

Rose looked down at her bowl and to her amazement, she found it was empty.

"More?" asked Kye.

"Please."

"Eloo?"

Eloo, however, was not listening. Her luminescent eyes had gone distant and her voice, when she answered, seemed to come from a distance.

"No thank you, Kye, I don't want any breakfast."

"Panther, come back to us for a moment, it's dinner time, not breakfast, so do you want soup or not?"

Eloo's eyes focused on the werewolf and she smiled apologetically.

"Sorry, Kye, I was thinking about the fireflower potion."

"I took it off the boil, when I did the soup."

"But is it ready?"

Kye growled back in his throat, and Rose glanced at him, for it was not a human sound.

"Of course it is, you've been brewing it since last night, remember."

"Have I?" Eloo asked, as if this was a complete surprise to her. Catching the look of bemusement on Rose's face, Eloo laughed. For a moment Rose thought she was being played with, but Eloo's words put her right.

"Sorry, my dear, it's the look on your face. Though I am not laughing at you! I must explain I am driven by my air nature and it means I sometimes get distracted away from something I was doing. But I always come back to it in the end."

"If it hasn't boiled over by then."

"What was that, my dear?" Eloo asked, as if she hadn't heard.

Though with ears like hers, she couldn't have missed it.

Kye did not reply, but disappeared to prepare more bowls of the steaming soup. While he was gone, Rose struggled (with Eloo's help) out of the hammock and into her dress. Rose noticed the dress had been repaired. The gash had been closed with green thread hiding the repair, and most of the red stain of her blood had been washed out of the green cotton. As she struggled into the dress, she felt Eloo's eyes on her body and she blushed.

"There is nothing to be ashamed about, my dear. You have a lovely body, you should be proud of it."

"I'm sorry, but I can't bear to show off my body like, like…"

"Like me?"

Rose nodded, looking down a little shame faced. She was proud of her body and had every right to be. She was tall for a woman, almost six feet, with long, supple legs and strong, toned muscles, which she had worked hard to develop. She, like her sister, had trained long in the fighting circle, to train herself in the arts of war. She had a good pair of breasts, though they were no competition for Eloo's. Her face was pretty, if a little too masculine, with a firm jaw and broad cheekbones. Still, she had been taught to be a lady at court. The thought of prancing around naked, like this elf girl, was foreign to her.

However, these were matters to be dealt with later. There were other problems to be addressed first, like how weak she was. She felt weak and shakier than she would have believed possible and was wondering how she would stand. Eloo, who must have had the same thoughts, wrapped her arm around Rose's waist and supported her as she hobbled along on jelly legs. Eloo led her through the tree house to where a low table projected from the planks. Gathering many pillows, Eloo made up a kind of seat for Rose, who gratefully sank into their comfort.

"Are you sitting comfortably, then I shall begin?" joked Eloo, and Rose realised the half smile which was always tugging at the girl's lips, was not just for her benefit, but was always there, just waiting for an opportunity to break out into a wide grin.

"I am very comfortable," Rose answered, though to be truthful she still felt dizzy and weak. Could this be the enchantment her nurse had always warned her about?

"When you've had some food, you'll feel stronger and we'll see if I have something to buck you up."

"Have we met before," she heard herself ask, though she had not been aware of forming the thought.

Eloo hesitated, considering the question. Then she shook her black maned head and laughed brightly. "I am sure I would have remembered it, but why do you ask?"

"I don't know, it's just a feeling that I have seen you before somewhere."

"Where is your home?"

"Just outside Landon."

"It has been at least thirty years, since I have been south," Eloo said, her smile vanishing for a moment. A dark look floated like a cloud across the sun of her face, then it was gone. "So I don't think we can have met."

Kye appeared then, laying steaming bowls before Rose and Eloo. In the centre of the table he placed a half loaf of bread and a wooden cup bearing some steaming liquid.

"What's that?"

"Mulled wine. Drink it while it's warm and you'll feel right as rain."

Rose reached for it and raising it to her lips, was washed in a wave of strong spices, which made her head spin a little. She had drunk mulled wine before, but there was something about this draught which spoke to her in ways she had not thought possible. As she stared into its dark depths, she felt she could hear a strong wind blowing and the spices changed to the smell of burning wood smoke and she heard as if from a distance the howling of wolves.

She was wondering whether she should drink this wine, when she felt the hot liquor hit the back of her throat and gasped in shock. The liquor was warm, but not scalding. No, it was the taste which made her gasp and shudder. The wine was strong and filled with the taste of spices she could not name or identify, but the overall effect was the glow of fire. Not a burning sensation, but the warm glow of a banked fire's heat after the bracing cold of a winter's air.

"It's good, no?" Eloo grinned, slapping Rose on the back. "Kye brews it and it's good stuff. It will take hairs off your chest."

"Or put them on," Kye said, handing Eloo another cup of the steaming liquor.

Rose set the cup down, and tried to steady herself on the table. However, once she had recovered from the initial shock, she had to admit she felt a little stronger.

"Thank you," she managed to sputter.

She was surprised to see a broad grin light up his dark face. She realised that, like many dogs, his bark was worse than his bite.

"You're welcome, fire child."

Rose looked up from her bowl at this, a look of startled surprise written on her face.

"What did you call me?"

"Fire child," Kye said, his dark penetrating eyes boring into her.

"What is it?" Eloo asked Rose, seeing the shock on her face.

"My mother called me that when I was knee high! How do you know it?"

Rose had looked down at her bowl, but she quickly glanced up in time to see a quick knowing glance pass between the two fey folk.

"What, what is it, what do you know about me?"

"The name's appropriate," Kye said, pointing at her flaming red hair.

Rose was now wary of the two; she lowered her eyes back to the bowl and continued to eat. However, she searched her heart, like her father had always told her to do when troubled. She felt they were not evil, but perhaps they did know more about her than they were letting on, but if this was the case why would they not tell her?

"Any more wine?"

Rose shook her head, and using the bread to wipe up the last dregs of the stew, she leant back against the piled cushions and stared up at the moving leaves.

Eloo began to sing, some wordless tune. A soft croon, which somehow made Rose think of bells tinkling, like wind chimes in a gentle breeze. As Rose half closed her eyes the leaves became clouds and the clouds became pictures from her past.

A smile slid across her pouted lips as her father appeared above her and smiled down at her. She did not cry now, she was too sleepy and calm to cry. Her feeling of peace increased when her mother appeared beside him, her smile lighting up Rose's memory, and she slipped into the deep healing arms of oblivion.

Kye watched her and only when gentle snores began to creep from her mouth, did he turn to where Eloo was watching her with a searching stare.

"Could she be?"

"She is about the right age, and it might explain Kain's involvement."

"Kain!"

"Yes, Kain. Oh Kye, this girl's sister could be in very great danger."

"I am ahead of you. Bright Eyes is looking into it."

Eloo's irrepressible smile broke out, like the sun from behind a cloud.

"Oh my darling Kye, I love you because you think of everything."

She leapt into his arms and wrapping her long legs around his waist, she began to squirm against him.

"Don't you think of anything else?" he growled at her, as though he was not interested.

"Yes, but then I become horny again," she said, wriggling against him. "So are you going to bed me, or not?"

"I should tie you up and then you wouldn't take up my time!"

He acted as if he was not interested, though Eloo could feel his body was saying yes, even if he wasn't.

"Oh, that sounds good," she said reaching under his tunic. "I don't mind being tied up, so long as you make love to me while you're doing it."

Kye snarled, as if in exasperation, but he carried her to their bed.

THE WOLF WITHIN

"The Werewolf is a creature who is always at war with the beast. There are times when the Wolf within must be let loose, if the man is to keep his sanity."
From the introduction to the Book of The Wolf.

When Rose came around this time, she knew where she was, which was useful, as it was now dark under the leaves. There was, however, a kind of star beneath the leaves, a star giving off the familiar scent of tobacco. She half rose on her elbow, to see a few feet away Kye's long face, partially lit by the red eye of a pipe.

"That reminds me of home."

"You smoke?"

"No, but my father does... did, and it reminds me of him."

"Good, smoking isn't good for you. I don't usually," he said around the pipe's stem, "but I use it to calm me and it is near full moon."

Rose looked at the grey hair, illuminated by the pipe's light and decided she should ask the question that had been burning away at her, ever since seeing his wolf like face.

"I hope you don't mind me asking, but do you always look, well, like this?"

Kye's eyes glinted yellow at her, then he took the pipe from his mouth and gave a bark of laughter.

"Well, aren't you a bold one?"

"Well?"

"Why do you ask?"

"I seem to remember glimpsing you before when I was hurt, only I don't remember all the hair..."

He laughed again and after taking another drag on the pipe, answered her. "You are quite correct. I didn't have so much hair then, but that was a new moon, and it is nearly full now."

"I still don't understand."

"The closer the moon gets to full, the closer the wolf comes."

Rose would like to have asked more, but his unusual talkativeness had ceased and he would not say another word for the moment.

She sank back into the cushions and tried to make sense of what he had just told her. If she understood him, the closer the moon came to full, the more the wolf that was part of his nature came to the fore and the man became less and less. This was why he was smoking, in an attempt to calm the wolf and maintain his humanity. However, if this was so did it make him less safe? Was he safe to be around in such a state? Then again, was she safe with either of these mysterious beings? She did not know them, and yet they had bound her wound, fed her and seemed to mean her no harm. If they did want something from her, she could not imagine what it could be.

"Where is...Eloo?"

Kye did not answer with words, but instead pointed with the pipe's stem towards a hanging and Rose guessed she might be asleep.

"More mulled wine?"

"No thank you. I don't suppose there is any news of Robin?"

"Not yet," Kye grunted.

Rose was about to ask him another question, when the calm of the night was torn apart by the long, blood chilling call of a wolf. She had been told how it spoke to the instincts of fear, but being told something and experiencing it are never the same thing! She was just recovering from it, when Kye uttered an animal like snarl and leapt to his feet.

"By the blood moon, what now?"

"It was a wolf..."

"I know that, girl, it was the rally cry."

This made no sense to Rose at all, but she had little chance to ask him more as he was gone. The only trace of his existence was a dissipating cloud of smoke and a swinging door hanging. Rose was wondering what she would do, when another hanging moved and the cat woman emerged. Her large green eyes (which were definitely glowing green in the dim light), blinked sleepily.

"Did I hear a wolf cry?"

"Yes, Kye said something about the rally or something."

This news changed Eloo's demeanour at once. She stiffened and her ears pricked up. Her tail, which was always flicking about her, went still. Though Rose did not know the woman well, she could tell her news had startled the elf.

"What is it?"

"Trouble."

With these words, Eloo followed Kye through the hanging.

With an effort, Rose pulled herself out of the cushions and padded after the lovers. She found Eloo standing at the top of a rope ladder, looking down at the ground. Rose came up to stand alongside the small woman and looked down, to see Kye standing among a pack of four or five wolves. The largest, a great grey beast with a white flash along its back, was at Kye's feet and as far as Rose could tell the werewolf and the wolf were talking to one another. Kye was barking at the wolf and the wolf was growling back when he paused.

"Is he doing what I think he's doing?"

"Kye is talking to Fang," Eloo said matter of factly as if telling Rose the weather was damp.

Rose was about to ask her what they were talking about when the pack broke up and, following the leader, loped away into the trees, leaving Kye looking after them. Rose could not see his face, but she could tell by his spear straight stance that the news was not good.

"What is it?"

"A Fire Dragon," Kye snarled, as he turned and swung himself up the ladder.

"Where, here?"

"To the south," Kye said, scrambling up onto the platform.

"A dragon?" Rose asked, not quite believing her ears. She had heard of them of course, but thought they were myths. "I thought there were none left."

"There aren't, perhaps, as many as there should be, but there are still a few of them in the world. The problem is that they are not always a force for good."

"This one is burning where he goes," Kye said, brushing past them.

"It's evil then?"

"Evil?" Eloo considered this for a long time before she answered. "Evil is probably too simple a statement. Dragons are a force unto themselves. Some might be called good, some evil, and some are just following their natures. Would you call the earthquake evil?"

"So why is Kye in such a rush?"

"Because the council has ruled against this dragon," came Kye's voice from within the tree house. "Eloo, are you coming or not?"

"In just a minute."

"So you're going to kill this dragon?"

"Not if we can help it. We might be able to persuade him to go back to sleep or go elsewhere."

"Go back to sleep?"

Rose opened her mouth to ask another question when Kye's voice came from within the tree house.

"Eloo we need to leave now, if we are to make it to the hall in time for the gathering."

"Coming," Eloo said, and she dashed away, leaving Rose wondering whether this matter involved her.

A moment later Kye appeared, carrying a longbow. On his back he wore a light pack. An arrow bag hung at one hip and a short sword at the other.

"Are you coming or staying?"

"What is this hall?"

"You shall see when you get to it, and I shall tell you now that you will not speak of it to anyone else."

Rose felt intimidated by this statement and she saw at once that wherever this place was it was a secret meeting place of the fey folk.

"Do you trust me, then?"

"I do not need to trust you," was Kye's cryptic answer, but before another word could pass between them Eloo appeared behind him.

"Kye, don't browbeat the poor girl!"

Rose saw that Eloo had put on a short dress of dark green and belted a long slim sword over this. She, too, was carrying a small pack.

"Are we ready?"

"I need my father's sword."

Kye turned and returned with her sword and a pair of sandals, which Rose had been wearing when she set out on that terrible morning.

"These will have to do for now," he said, passing them to her. "We will see what we can fit you with, at the hall."

"How far is it?"

"About an hour's march," Eloo said. "Or perhaps less, as the wolf runs."

"Fang and his pack have gone to scout before us," Kye said, as if in reply to an unspoken question from Eloo.

"But how will we see our way through a dark wood?"

"Kye is our guide tonight," Eloo said, leading Rose to the ladder.

"Can he see in the dark?"

"Yes," was his growl, from the ladder's foot.

Once they hit the forest floor, Kye was off through the trees, his tall form disappearing in front of them. He set a quick pace, which Rose was hard put to keep up, as her wound had weakened her considerably. Eloo strode beside her, never leaving her side and as she, too, could see in the dark, she told Rose where large roots broke up the track. Rose was flagging when they came to a halt and she realised the dark, impenetrable wall of trees was lightening. As they slowly moved forwards, they emerged into a large clearing, bright with moonlight. Rose realised Kye stood before them, his form rigid, his shaggy head thrown back, his eyes locked on the moon. As she watched he let loose a great and blood chilling wolf like cry.

"What's wrong with him?"

"The wolf within wants to be let loose," Eloo said, before dashing to Kye's side. "Kye, it's fine. If you want to go I can carry your gear."

Kye, Rose saw, had drawn a long, silver chain from within his tunic and was gripping some medallion on the end with a death grip.

He shook his head.

"I must be able to say the passwords or the Wards will not let us pass."

"But you can do that when we get there and I can change you back for that, but between there and here you can run as a wolf."

Kye seemed to have to concentrate hard to understand what Eloo was telling him. For a long time, all he could do was stand there, staring at the moon, and pant, his whole body shaking. Then he tore the chain from around his neck and gave it to Eloo before he darted away, into the trees. A moment later a great, black wolf emerged from where he had gone. Its huge form glistened, the silver flash marking Kye's hairline shining in the moonlight.

"That's Kye?" Rose asked, watching with trepidation, as the huge wolf approached. His mouth was open, a long tongue hanging out and he panted as he came to a halt at Eloo's feet. His shoulder overtopped her head.

Rose watched with interest as the large wolf and Eloo rubbed cheeks, and to her amazement the wolf and the elf kissed or at least touched each other's mouth. Though Rose would never let the wolf get anywhere that close.

"This is Kye the wolf," Eloo said, stroking the dark fur beneath its jaw. "Wolf Kye, this is Rose, Rose, this is wolf Kye," she continued, drawing Rose's hand to the wolf's nose as though introducing Rose to Kye as if they had never met, which when Rose thought about it, she supposed they were meeting for the first time as wolf and woman.

Rose wanted to drag her hand from Eloo's, for she was afraid to have it near the wolf's fangs, which glittered like icicles in the moonlight, but she was afraid of startling the beast.

To her surprise the wolf's huge tongue touched her hand and withdrew. The wolf looked up at her with those yellow eyes and Rose saw within their wild storm of primitive emotions a spark of more than animal intelligence. She realised that she still had a sense of the man who had cared for her. The wolf huffed at her and then it turned and growled, its hackles standing erect, its hair bristling.

LIGHTNING AND CLOUD

"NEVER JUDGE a Wereding by its cover."
Takana the Harpy.

Eloo and Rose both reached for their swords understanding Kye was not growling at them, but at something they could not see, which he had detected. They looked in the direction in which his crinkled muzzle was pointing.

Then to their relief his hackles smoothed, his growl changed to a high whine and he was off and running, his tail wagging in great sweeps. They watched him go before exchanging glances.

"It appears that he knows who it is," Eloo said, and let her half drawn sword slide back into its sheath. "Shall we go and see?"

They followed Kye's swishing tail to find him standing on his hind legs licking the face of a tall, wiry man who was almost being pulled down by the wolf.

"Enough, enough Kye, you're drowning me," the man cried in a surprisingly gravelly voice for such a gangly figure.

"Lightning," Eloo cried, in obvious delight.

"Eloo, would you please call Kye off, he's killing me here!"

When Kye dropped back onto all fours, Rose saw the man who both Kye and Eloo knew was a tall, gangling figure dressed in a dark cloak and high boots. His face, which was clearly lit by the moon, was long and narrow with a thin beak of a nose and large green eyes blinking in the light. They widened to huge pools when they lit on Rose.

"And who is this?"

"Rose, may I present Lightning, a student of the fire school."

The man made Rose laugh despite herself, as with a dramatic gesture he swept the floppy hat he wore off his head and made a dramatic bow.

"Lightning Flamespeaker, third circle of the fire school, at your service!"

"Charmed, I'm sure," Rose said. Although she should be grave and curtsey back, the man's manner of casual flippancy made it impossible to keep a silly grin off her face as she accepted his proffered hand.

The hand was like the man, long and thin, but it was worn and calloused. As he withdrew it, she noticed he wore a large gold ring on his middle finger. This ring glowed in the bright moonlight and Rose saw it bore a rune or Sigel on it, but it was withdrawn before she could get a good look at it.

"You have heard of the Fire Dragon?" Eloo asked, looking him up and down, taking in the walking stick he was leaning on and the short sword hanging from his belt.

"I am making for the hall. When I heard Kye's cry I angled in this direction."

"You came on foot from the eyrie?" Eloo asked, her voice showing disbelief.

"No, of course not. I was at my tower, a few miles north when the call came, so I saddled Cloud and here I am." When Lightning referred to Cloud, he pointed with his walking stick and Rose saw a few yards away a black stallion grazing the long grass, its head raising to whinny when it heard its name.

"That is fortunate," Eloo gushed, her hands clapping in joy. "You can carry Rose, while I go ahead with Kye."

"Always glad to be of service," Lightning said, a wide grin lighting up his lean face.

"Good, then I'll get Kye's gear. You can take some of it on Cloud if he's not too loaded already."

"Certainly not," Lightning said, faking hurt.

Lightning gave a low whistle and the horse stopped its cropping, gave a soft whinny and trotted across to stand next to its master. It was then that Rose saw how very large it was, head level with its master, though it seemed to have a good nature as it whinnied and nuzzled Lightning's shoulder. Lightning, for his part, stroked the horse's velvety neck and whispered something to it. The horse turned on Rose a large and intelligent eye.

"Cloud, this is Rose and you, she and I are all going to be good friends, aren't we?"

In response the horse snorted, and turning towards Rose, thrust its head forward. Rose thought it was going to bite her, but a second later she realised the big horse was simply sniffing her. She knew about horses and cautiously extended a hand to the black's muzzle.

The horse sniffed, whinnied softly and the next instance Rose was almost bowled over, as the horse thrust its head at her and rubbed at her shoulder.

"He likes you," Lightning said, laughter bubbling up in his voice. "Let's see if he'll carry you?"

Before Rose knew what was happening, Lightning had slid forwards and with a strength belying his wiry appearance, lifted her up and placed her on the broad leather saddle on the horse's back.

Rose grabbed for the reins, as Cloud reared beneath her, a neigh escaping his mighty lungs. The horse was already moving when Rose realised what had happened and its quick gallop round the clearing was over before it had begun. Before she could take in the horse was moving, Cloud was back standing in front of Lightning. His nostrils flared as he huffed and snorted.

"I'm not sure he likes me up here," Rose said, and she tried to bring the horse's head closer, only to have the reins jerked from her hands.

"He likes it fine. What he doesn't like is you trying to keep him on a short rein. They're for you to stay on the saddle, not to control him, he knows what he's doing."

Rose nodded, seeing at once what he meant. Gathering the reins up in her hands, she kept them in a loose grip, so Cloud could have his head.

"Are we ready?" Eloo asked, and passed Kye's pack and longbow to Lightning.

"I think so," Lightning replied, strapping the pack onto Cloud's saddle and hefted the bow, which was slightly taller than him.

"Then lead on, Kye."

With a low grunt, the wolf turned from where it had been cocking its leg against a tree and with a swish of his black brush he disappeared into the black wall of the trees.

"Perhaps if you give me the reins I can lead Cloud," Lightning said, grinning up at her.

"Can you see in the dark, too?"

"I have a good nose."

Rose did not comment on this as Lightning took the reins from her and she looked up at the approaching trees, half expecting to be struck by low hanging branches as they entered the all but impenetrable darkness, but it was apparent that the branches, if there were any, were high above her head. She was left with the impression of travelling through a great hall with the branches forming the rafters of such a structure.

For a long time they travelled like this and Rose was lulled by the gentle swaying of the horse. She was beginning to nod off when once more the darkness gave way to a glowing moonlit clearing. This time, however, the space stretching before Rose was much larger than the clearing they had just left. The land before them was a low valley, clear of trees, which fell gently to where a broad river shone silver in the moonlight.

"The Trespasser, they call it," Lightning said from beside the horse's head.

"Kye tells me that it is, or was, called the Trant or Trent, or something like that in ancient times," Eloo said, from where she stood just in front, her eyes on the wolf standing at the river's edge.

"But it has been called the Trespasser for hundreds of years! How does Kye know this other name?" Rose asked, her sleepiness gone.

Eloo turned to face her and gave her a long, searching glance. "I'm not sure Kye would thank me for telling you this...How old do you think Kye is, Rose?"

"Thirty," Rose said and then stopped, thinking back to those ageless eyes.

"Kye is over three hundred years old," Eloo said. "And besides, he has access to his past lives."

Rose, however, did not understand this. Plus, she was reeling from the realisation that the being who had nursed her was so old.

"How?"

"He's a werewolf," Lightning said, noticing her amazement.

Rose went to ask him what he meant, when Wolf Kye hurled back its head and gave a long howl. This was eerie enough, but seconds later, from the dark wall of trees atop the opposite valley wall there came a number of answering howls, making Rose realise they were going to meet a large number of wolves and maybe werewolves. She shivered in her saddle as she examined her feelings about that.

"We're going to meet other werewolves?"

"We're going to the hall, of course we're going to meet werewolves," Lightning said, leading Cloud to the river edge.

As they reached it, Eloo was hanging the silver chain round the wolf's neck. A second later the wolf was gone and Kye's naked and shivering form was squatting in its place. Eloo wrapped her cloak round his shoulders and whispered in his ear.

"Lightning, can you explain something to me?"

"If I can."

"Why is Kye struggling with his change? I thought werewolves could change at will?"

"They can, and they don't need the full moon to do it, but the wolf is ruled by the phases of the moon. As it moves to full the wolf becomes dominant over the man and it becomes harder to keep a man's form. Especially if a werewolf like Kye has held the change off for a long time."

"Why would he do that?"

"So he can spend time with Eloo, rather than hunting with the pack."

THE WOLF'S LAIR

"Werewolves are pack creatures, they have extended families that will stake a claim to a place of natural beauty and dedicate it to their goddess."
The Book of the Wolf.

Rose might have asked more questions, but her attention was drawn to Kye and the river. As she watched him approach the water a mist sprang up from nowhere, and thickened into a wall of fog. Kye's form was silhouetted against the white wall and she could see him making gestures with one hand, while he held up the chain in the other. Something on the end of it shimmered in the dim light, and as quickly as it had appeared the mist was gone, leaving the broad river chuckling before them, clear of mist and any other obstacles. At least it seemed so, for Kye waded forwards and onto the south bank, where he performed more rites.

"Is he casting a spell?" Rose felt both thrilled and worried by the fact she was watching what in her world was illegal.

"A spell, not quite. He is performing the rites and rituals that will allow us to pass the protective magics the clan have woven around the hall. If Kye or another member of the pack were not with us, we would struggle to pass this point."

"Why? What kind of magic protects this hall?"

"I don't know," Lightning said, smiling up at her. "It's a closely guarded secret."

Seconds later, Lightning led Cloud into the water and before Rose could get her boots wet they were on the other bank. Rose expected them to proceed into the trees, but before they did Kye knelt before two great oaks, which with their massive interlinking branches formed an arch into the darkness. Here a huge spider's web hung before them. Kye touched the network of silver strands and spoke something in a whisper and the curtain of silk was gone, as if it had never existed. Rose wanted to ask Lightning what had just happened, but they were moving forwards already.

Once they were under the trees she glanced back to see the net of gossamer strands standing out against the moonlight. She realised that although it looked like a spider's web, it was in reality protective magic Kye had removed so they could pass.

"Are there any more wards?" Rose asked in a whisper, feeling the darkness press down on her.

"No wards," replied Kye's hoarse voice. "But the woods are not unguarded."

They progressed in silence for a few more minutes and then they emerged into a small clearing, hazily lit by moonlight falling between large branches.

"This is where we leave Cloud," Lightning said, as he tied the horse's reins to a low hanging branch.

Rose slid off the saddle and Lightning helped her. She was about to ask Lightning something when two grey shadows ran from the darkness of the trees. Gasping in fear Rose reached for her sword as the grey shadows rushed towards Kye. However, as she grasped the hilt of her sword Lightning's hand gently held her arm.

"It's fine, Rose, these are friends."

As Rose watched, Kye dropped to one knee and the grey shadows leapt at him. She drew in a breath, expecting to see blood fly into the air, but the wolves merely licked Kye's face. Kye, for his part, made a low growling sound and ruffled the hair of the two wolves.

"Rose, please come here," Kye said, his yellow eyes fixed on the wolves' eyes.

Rose hesitated for a moment, but sharing a look with Lightning she did as the werewolf asked. When she reached Kye he looked up at her, and taking her hands held them out to the wolves.

Rose closed her eyes, half expecting to feel fangs fasten on her hands, but instead she felt the rough warmth of their tongues.

"Lea, Lor, this is Rose, a new friend. See her, smell her and know her for a friend."

Rose opened her eyes to see the wolves sniffing at her hands. She glanced into Kye's glittering eyes and saw an expression of pleased amusement.

"Rose, may I present you to my youngest brothers, Lea and Lor."

"Pleased to meet them," Rose said, releasing a breath she had not been aware of holding.

"I said there were no more wards, but there are guards," Kye said, tapping the wolves heads.

"What of the rest of the pack?" Eloo asked.

"They await us within the hall itself," Kye said, rising, his eyes looking down at the wolves. "Eloo, I am sorry, but the pack calls to me..."

"Then go to them, Kye, we have passed the wards. The pack will either let us enter or it won't, and you can better help us as a wolf than a man."

Kye gave her a grim smile and held out the chain to Eloo, who caught it as it fell from his hand which was no longer a hand. Rose turned to look at Kye, both afraid and amazed, for this was the first time she had witnessed a werewolf change. She half expected Kye to howl in agony as his bones ground against one another and reshaped themselves, but the change happened in the blink of an eye. One minute Kye was a man, the next (with a faint shimmer that made his form look as though it was being seen through smoke or water), he was the huge black wolf that did howl now, but it sounded to Rose's untutored ears like a howl of joy rather than pain.

"Lead on, Kye," Eloo said, hanging the chain about her neck.

Kye the wolf moved forwards and the two grey wolves took up flanking positions, as they led them into the darkness of the trees.

"Lightning, what is that chain that keeps Kye in human form?" Rose asked as the party moved eastwards.

"At a guess, I would say it was Kye's badge of rank in the Silver Shield," was Lightning's response, and he gently took hold of her arm and led her into the shade of the trees.

"The Silver Shield, what is that?"

"In the fire's name! Do they teach you nothing about our people in the human world?"

"Actually, no, they don't. All I know about werewolves is they change at the full moon into monsters that will stop at nothing to hunt you down."

"Well, we will have to re-educate you. The Silver Shield is the Elven king's personal bodyguard. They protect the Elven people."

Rose wanted to ask more questions, but she was distracted by the avenue of trees which she now entered. Before her there was a thirty foot spread of green sward running up between twin columns of oaks and ashes that must be ancient for they were hundreds of feet tall. Their branches entwined to create a roof high above her head to form natural hall. Sitting between the columns was every size and colour of wolf, their yellow eyes glinting at her from among the shadows.

Kye paid them no attention, but led them up the middle of the columned trees to where a huge tree stump sat between them. Here, on this wooden table, there glittered silver items, but Rose was not able to take them in for she was fixed by the two wolves sitting on either side of this stump. So far she had thought Kye was the largest wolf in existence. Certainly he was larger than any wolf she had glanced at between the trees, but the two wolves waiting silently for them at the stump were larger than she thought wolves could possibly grow.

They were probably the height of her father's warhorse and rippled with muscle. The one on Rose's left was a huge black whose fur was even darker than Kye's and was nearly as dark as Eloo's hair, but on its chest there was a broad flash of white that resembled a crescent.

The wolf on the other side was slightly smaller than the black and Rose guessed this might be a bitch wolf. The wolf was still huge. She, too, was all but black, but her head was almost covered in a silver sheen Rose had only seen on Kye's brow, and guessed this wolf might be his mother. Kye went up to the wolf with the flash and lay down before him, his ears lowered, his whine sounding almost like a plea. The black wolf lowered its head and touched Kye's silver brow with its chin. Kye got up slowly and moved back, his tail between his legs, his head lowered in submission.

"Rose, you had better come and be introduced to Flash and Great Mother," Eloo said, and took Rose by the arm, pulling her towards the huge wolf pair.

Rose opened her mouth to protest, but before she could she was standing before the wolf with the silver head. This wolf stared into her eyes with a pair that were not yellow, but a startling blue, reminding Rose of Kye in his human form.

"Great Mother," Eloo said with a curtsey. "May I introduce Rose, a young person of whom I think you have heard."

The huge wolf, who Eloo referred to as Great Mother, took a large step forwards and lowering its huge muzzle sniffed at Rose. The wolf huffed and stepped back. Eloo turned Rose to meet the glowing yellow eyes of the huge black wolf.

"My lord Flash," Eloo said with a slightly shallower bow, "May I present Rose to you. She is the girl your son and I found at the passing place."

The huge wolf did not come near, but cocked its head and after giving Rose a long look, huffed and turned away as if dismissing her.

"Okay, that's enough introductions, let's step back," said Lightning from behind them and Rose felt his hand on her shoulder, drawing her back from the stump. "Let's let them get on with their business."

Rose was only too happy to draw back from these huge beasts.

As they did, the wolf Eloo had called Flash hurled back his head and gave a huge howl, echoed by the rest of the pack behind Rose, their cries turning her blood to ice. Eloo pulled Rose and Lightning to one side and as she did the whole pack pawed past them, streaming past the wooden stump and through an arch of branches out into the silver light of the moon Rose could see beyond it.

"Where are they going?"

"To hunt," Eloo said, staring after them. "Only tonight they hunt for the Fire Dragon."

Rose heard a note of concern in Eloo's voice and looking round, realised Kye had disappeared with the rest of the pack.

"What will they do if they find it?"

"They might attack it," Lightning said. "But I doubt it."

"Why?"

"Because a Fire Drake is usually too large and powerful even for a pack of werewolves."

"I hope you are right, Lightning," Eloo sighed, her eyes glistening with unshed tears.

Lightning tried to take Eloo's mind off the pack by proposing they eat. He produced bread, cheese, fruit and ale from his pack and they sat at the foot of some of the trees and ate in silence, as they thought their separate thoughts. However, Rose could not hold her curiosity any longer, and had to ask the questions bubbling up.

"Eloo, what exactly is this place?"

"This is the hall, the clan hall, their meeting place and ritual temple. Though most rites are held at the silver temple over there." Eloo made a gesture in an easterly direction.

"So when will they return?"

"Probably not till dawn," Eloo guessed, "so we might as well get some sleep while we are waiting for them."

Rose didn't like to say, but she didn't like the idea of going to sleep only to wake to find a pack of werewolves standing over her. Still, she couldn't find the words to express this. So she allowed Eloo to lead her through the columns to where a large bundle of animal skins and branches had been laid to make a bed.

"You and I shall lie here," Eloo said, unbelting her sword, and without another word she flung herself onto the bed, her body curling into a tight ball.

Rose considered what to do, and after unstrapping her sword she placed it within easy reach and lay on the furs that were surprisingly comfortable. She was obviously more tired than she had realised, for she had not expected to sleep, but as soon as she lay her head on her arm she fell into a deep sleep.

THE SILVER LADY

"The Lady speaks to us through dreams and visions. This is because the mortal mind cannot behold her beauty and survive."
From the Book of the Wolf.

Her sleep, however, was not dreamless, for during that night she had the most vivid dream she had ever experienced.

In her dream she woke to find herself not in the Hall, but the most beautiful gardens she had ever seen. She had been to the royal gardens at Landon's royal palace and thought they were the best, but even they were not as beautiful as these gardens. All about her were trees bearing large multi-coloured flowers and fruit like silvered plums.

The gardens were lit with a silvery light pouring from silver lanterns looking like mini moons. Rose wandered through the gardens seeing tiny birds and large snakes move out of her way. She was beginning to believe the garden was deserted of human life when she came upon a large pool. Bathing within its waters was a woman, or at least that was what she appeared to be, for her silhouette was all Rose could make out. The woman was surrounded by an ever shifting halo of silvery light, as if she was illuminated by the moon's rays which moved as clouds moved across them.

"Please, Rose, come closer, I am your friend," came the woman's voice from among this shifting light. A gentle and kind voice, it made Rose feel as though a soft rain or a gently flowing stream had found a voice.

Rose came closer and as she did she saw on the lake's bank silver clothing and what looked like a shield made of silver.

"Who are you?"

"My servant Kye would call me the Silver Lady, but to you I shall be known as Selene."

"What are you?"

"At the moment, Rose, that does not matter!"

"What does matter?"

"That you take a message back with you."

46

"Back, back where?"

"Back to the waking world. You are dreaming, Rose, but none of that matters just now. What matters is my message."

"To whom should I give this message?"

"To any who will listen, but I think Kye will be the most useful ear. He has proved most useful in the past."

"Useful?"

"Please, Rose, we have so little time, even as we speak Kye comes to wake you. The message is this, Kye and my priests must look to the prophecies of the Grey Pilgrim. If they do not the Elven people will be wiped out."

"But why can't you tell them what you want to?"

"Because it is not in my power to interfere directly in events. I must act through others like you."

"But why me?"

"Because, my lovely Rose, it is as much your destiny as my own that I act to protect."

Rose was completely taken aback, for this woman was saying she had a destiny, but even as this idea broke over her, so too was the feeling of the dream slipping away. With this, the image of the woman began to fade into a silver mist. "Remember, Rose," came the silky voice, as if from a distance, "The prophecies of the Grey Pilgrim."

THE PROPHECIES OF THE GREY PILGRIM

"When the silver Lady is imprisoned, her people will be crushed.
Unless the cleaved mirror is mended, they will be lost."

The Prophecies of the Grey Pilgrim.

Rose woke to find not a pack of ravening werewolves standing over her, but simply Kye crouching at her side, his calloused hand gently shaking her shoulder. When Rose met his eyes they were blue, and for some reason she could not explain (for she had not seen the lady's eyes), they made her remember the woman's words.

"Kye, you must look in the prophecies of the Grey Pilgrim."

Kye's eyes widened before narrowing in suspicion. "How do you even know of those writings?"

"I don't know about them," Rose said as she pulled a cloak about her, for the damp of early morning was in the air. "She told me to tell you that message."

"She?"

"Sel... she said you knew her as the Silver Lady."

"The Silver Lady gave you this message to pass on to me?"

"Well, she said anyone who would listen, but yes, she did mention your name."

Kye shook his head, seemingly overwhelmed by this revelation.

"What's wrong, don't you believe me?"

Kye appeared unable to answer her with words, though this might just have been his taciturn nature. He shook his head.

"Then what's wrong? Aren't I supposed to have conversations in my dreams or something?"

Kye again shook his head. His hand on her shoulder tightened its grip, Rose taking this to mean she should calm down. She took a deep breath, taking in with it the sweet smell of damp leaves and strong herbs. While she did this, Kye closed his eyes tightly and when Rose watched his lips she could have sworn he was forming words, though none reached her ears. Rose suspected (though she could not say how she knew it), Kye was somehow (perhaps with magic), communicating with someone else.

This suspicion was confirmed when a woman dressed in a dark green robe materialised next to them. Rose could tell this was one of Kye's sisters, for the resemblance was striking. Although the woman was shorter than Kye, she was still tall. Her shoulders were narrower than Kye's, but had the same stance. Her face was narrow, though with the wolf like look about it. However, even though she resembled Kye she was different. Her eyes were the feral yellow of the wolf and whereas Kye's temples were touched with silver, her waist long hair was almost completely a sheet of silver, save for one long braid of black hanging on her right shoulder. Rose noticed the wiry arms that hung loosely at her sides were covered in a sheen of silver fur.

"Rose, my sister, Silver Skin," Kye said, standing to his full height, revealing to Rose that he was naked save for a pair of leggings.

She stared at the steel cords of muscles running under his dark skin, which was marked by several scars crisscrossing his chest, noticing the grey hair protruding from his chest, belly and other places. She was not embarrassed this time, getting used to the fact these people did not care what they showed her, but she could not help asking as the question formed in her mind.

"Aren't you cold like that?"

Both Kye and the woman exchanged a look, then burst into laughter.

"What's so funny?"

"I'm sorry, Rose," Silver Skin said in a deep, almost masculine voice. "It's not you that we're laughing at, it's just that most people would be wondering why they were hanging about with werewolves, but you ask questions most people would not even dare to think let alone ask."

"And this makes you laugh?"

"I'm afraid so," Silver Skin said, and sat down on a nearby stump.

When she did, her robe opened slightly at the neck to reveal a variety of necklaces and charms, some appearing to be rawhide, others silver and gold. "To answer your question, no, Kye does not feel the cold as you do. His body has the vigour of werewolf blood running through it and this means we have a higher tolerance to cold, though, Kye, it might be a good idea to put something more on."

Kye did not reply to this, but was gone before Rose could even blink.

"How does he do that?"

"It's a gift," Silver Skin said, her wide mouth forming a sunburst of a smile. "Are you hungry?"

From beside Rose there came a long yawn and Eloo's voice purred in her ear. "Did someone mention food?"

"I might have known that would wake you, Eloo," Silver Skin laughed.

Eloo said something under her breath, but Rose did not catch it.

She was about to ask her what she said, when Kye came back, now dressed in tunic boots and a short cape. He was bearing a loaf of bread, cheese and a water skin.

"Sorry it's not hot," Silver Skin said as she broke the loaf, "but fire's not allowed within the Hall's precincts."

Rose shrugged and bit into the bread; it didn't matter, the food was wholesome enough. Lowering the water skin she met Silver Skin's yellow eyes and shivered. It was not the wolf like colour of those eyes that made her shiver, but the intensity of the stare. Rose felt as though the woman was staring into her soul and reading the thoughts on the back of her head.

"So tell me about this dream," Silver Skin said and took the water skin from Rose's hand.

Rose took a deep breath, and proceeded to repeat in as much detail as she could remember what happened in the dream. She was surprised to find she recalled almost every detail, something usually hard for her to do. Silver Skin listened in silence while Rose spoke, only gasping when Rose described her impression of the Silver Lady.

"Well, Silver, what do you make of it?" Kye asked, sharpening a long knife on a whetstone.

"Probably as much as you can yourself, Kye," Silver Skin answered after a long look skywards. "It is unusual for the Lady to give a sending to someone who is not a member of the priesthood, but it is not unheard of..."

"Heather," Kye breathed.

"Yes," Silver Skin said, a look of sympathy flitting across her face.

Rose was about to ask who Heather was, but Eloo interrupted.

"So do either of you know what these scrolls are?"

Kye and Silver exchanged a look that told Rose a silent conversation passed between them. Kye shrugged and Silver Skin nodded in agreement.

"They are a set of prophecies and predictions made by a figure known as the Grey Pilgrim."

"I have not heard of this," Eloo said, her purr implying she was considering what that meant.

"That does not surprise me, Eloo," Silver Skin said.

"Another of the tribe's secrets," Eloo said, cocking her head.

"Not this time," Kye said, his eyes meeting and locking with Eloo's. "The reason you have not heard of them, Eloo, is because they were written hundreds of years ago and have lain gathering dust ever since because although we have studied them, they have not yet been of use to us."

"Until now?" Eloo asked, her lopsided smile meant for Kye.

"So it would seem."

"So what are you going to do about it?" Rose asked.

"For the moment, nothing," Silver Skin said.

"Nothing?"

The female werewolf raised a hand to still Rose's amazed protest.

"The Fire Drake takes priority now, besides, the predictions are at the repository."

Spotting Rose's look of confusion, Silver Skin explained. "The repository is our library and seat of learning and is at least two days' travel from here.

"Once the Fire Drake is taken care of, I or Kye or one of the clan will consult the prophecies."

Rose sat quietly for a long moment, considering whether she was happy with this or not. She slowly became aware of the silence around her and looked up from her hands clasped in her lap to find Eloo, Kye and Silver Skin all watching her.

"Rose, if the Silver Lady had meant to tell us this was urgent she would have done so, but she has hinted that we must consult the records. This means there is still time to prevent this event, whatever it is," Silver Skin said, gently. "Please believe me, I have had such sendings myself and this is the one thing I have learnt from them. If the Lady means us to act upon them urgently she tells us directly."

Rose sighed and nodded.

"Speaking of the Fire Drake," Eloo broke in, "did you find any trace of him?"

"Nothing worth speaking of," Kye growled. "We found the trail of his devastation, but it stopped dead and he was nowhere to be found. It is as though he has left the area."

"Is that possible?"

"It could be, Rose, but I doubt it. I think he has become aware he is being hunted and has gone to ground to throw us off the scent."

"So what are we going to do?"

"We?" Silver Skin asked, raising an eyebrow. "By 'we' you include yourself?"

"Yes," Rose said, glaring at the woman. "Kye and Eloo brought me here! I thought it was to help with this dragon?"

"Perhaps it was, but now I wonder," Silver said, her eyes going far away, as though she was seeing something beyond Rose's vision.

"Well, what are we doing?"

"We are to break into small groups and sweep sections until we find it."

"From when?"

"As soon as we get properly armed," Silver said, "and speaking of armed, it would be better if Eloo and Rose had something more fitting to wear than dresses."

"The armoury is the next call."

"Is it just the four of us?"

THE ARMOURY

"The sharpest weapon is the mind."
Eloo, from the Wereding Chronicles by The Red Wizard.

Kye, as usual, did not answer with words, but rather used actions to answer Eloo's question. He gave a low whistle and from a nearby copse two figures materialised from among the shadows.

"Lea and Lor will be joining us," Silver said.

Rose turned her gaze to the two newcomers. They resembled Kye closely, having long black hair, though neither had any silver. They had the same wiry lithe look of their older brother about them, but as Kye stood and they moved with his animal grace to flank him on either side, she saw they were not quite as tall as him. Like their brother, they were dressed in tunics, boots and capes all dyed in browns and greens. They, too, held longbows and Rose saw they wore a collection of blades about their persons.

"You have an armoury here in the woods?"

"You'll see," Eloo said, and taking Kye's proffered hand came gracefully to her feet.

The small group, which was joined by Lightning as they passed back through the grove of the hall, returned to the river they had crossed the night before though Rose saw no sign of the web or the mist this time. They stayed on the hall side of the river and followed it downstream for about a hundred yards, until upon the right there rose a large tor, and it was towards this they headed.

Rose was about to ask Lightning, who was at her side, if they were going to enter through solid stone, when Kye bent to the low bank of grass and moss that rose gently to the vertical stone and pulled aside what appeared to be a door made of moss and grasses – and disappeared. Lea and Lor stood to either side flanking the door and standing guard, but Eloo and Silver Skin followed Kye into the low and dark entrance that lay before her.

"I'm supposed to go down there?"

"It's all right," Lightning reassured her. "I'll be behind you and it is lit further down."

Rose moved forward and found she had to almost bend double to fit through the small narrow opening, though beyond the door the tunnel grew higher and she could stand again. In the dim light Rose saw several broad steps carved into the stone and she hesitantly descended them. As she did she left the daylight behind but as she went deeper into the earth the light grew stronger rather than dimmer. Standing at the bottom of the steps she found herself in a large cave lit by torches burning with a cold blue light, which did not seem to give off any heat. The walls of this cavern were hung with every kind of weapon, from spears and longbows, to swords and great axes.

"What is this place?"

"This is the clan's armoury," Kye said as he removed a large shield emblazoned with a black wolf rampant.

Looking at the shield made Rose think about her coat of arms, the Canduss coat of arms, with a Golden Eagle standing on a red rose. The memory made her blink back tears as she remembered the colours fluttering above the house. To distract herself from her longing for her home, she looked at the many swords and shields lining the walls. Many of them were shaped in ancient designs, but all were designed to present the clan's symbol of a black wolf with a silver head. Its emblem reminded her of Great Mother's wolf form.

"Even my father's house didn't have this many weapons."

Kye grunted and turning, held out the shield to Rose.

"For me?"

"For you," Kye said, his blue eyes now hooded.

"But I am not a member of your clan."

"No, but you wish to carry arms against our enemies," Silver said, from where she was considering a brace of long knives. "That allows you certain privileges."

"Look at it this way, Rose," Eloo said, slipping her dress off to don a set of leathers. "You're an honorary member of the clan. I am a member of the clan only because I am Kye's lover, but I can use its arms so long as it is in the service of the clan."

"Or, as in this case, the realm," Silver said, strapping the knives about her narrow waist.

Rose did not know what to say, so instead she accepted the shield and holding it judged its weight. It was a good shield and looking up from it to thank Kye, she saw him holding out to her a set of leathers. She grabbed them out of the air as Kye lobbed them at her and found herself clutching a set of leathers in a mottled patchwork of brown and green. She glanced around, looking for somewhere she could change out of her dress and into these clothes, only to see Kye stripping and Eloo pulling up her leathers which she had just donned before all of them. She was panicking at the thought of stripping in front of them when Lightning tapped her on the shoulder and pointed out a small curtained alcove in one corner of the cave.

"You can change in there," he whispered conspiratorially in her ear.

"Thanks," she muttered and taking the shield and leathers she entered the alcove. Lightning drew the hanging shut behind her.

Rose slipped out of her dress and holding the leathers up to her body found they could have been made for her. The buckskin trousers were perhaps an inch too long, but a turn up would handle that. The leathers consisted of a pair of buckskin trousers and vest and a three quarter jacket of tanned leather. Rose was just tightening the rawhide laces when a hand holding a pair of tall hiking boots appeared round the curtain.

"Here, these should fit you," Eloo's voice said from the other side.

Rose caught them and found Eloo was right, they could have been made for her. She stepped out of the alcove to find Eloo now dressed in a set of skin tight leathers that were so figure hugging she might as well be naked. She was contemplating a four foot long staff, tipped with a six inch long bud like object.

"My Wand of Winds, I wondered what had happened to it!"

"You left it here last winter after you helped the clan drive the eclipsers out," Silver Skin said, as if Eloo should have remembered it.

"Did I?"

Lightning whistled when he saw Rose standing hesitantly in the alcove.

"Well, don't you look like a war goddess!"

Rose felt herself blushing as she looked down at her boots.

"Perhaps it is time we tested your arm," Silver Skin said, considering Rose over a six foot staff.

"Have we time?"

"Perhaps not, Kye, but you would not take a bad arrow to battle, now would you?"

"I have trained for years, I am not unskilled," Rose said.

"That we shall see," Silver said.

"Outside," Kye grunted.

They all trooped back up into the light and Kye led them to a wide, flat clearing, between the rock of the armoury and the wall of trees. Rose put her back to the rock, and with her shield on her arm drew her sword from its back sheath. She took a high guard and prepared to face an attack.

"Lea, you are about Rose's height, would you care to do the honours?" Silver Skin said, from where she stood with Kye and Eloo just under the boughs of the trees.

Rose watched as the tall werewolf drew from a back scabbard a long scimitar, which flashed in the sunlight when he flourished the blade.

She was bracing herself for his attack when Silver Skin spoke. "Wait, there is no need to hurt each other."

Both Rose and Lea turned, to find her holding a long branch in her hands.

"Bring me your blades, we shall make them safe to use."

Rose and Lea moved towards her and as they did, Silver Skin turned to the west and, drawing something shiny from beneath her robe, began to chant. Rose watched, fascinated, for although she had seen Kye clearing the road for them the night before, this was the first time she had properly seen the mythical magic of the Weredings. She was slightly disappointed when Silver Skin merely broke the branch in two and turning back to them touched their blades with the broken ends of the branch. She had been expecting something a little more dramatic.

"There, your blades are safe for now," the Druidess said, a slight smile on her lips.

Rose looked down to find to her surprise her blade had turned brown and taken on the appearance of wood. When she touched it, it was to find it was no longer metal, but wood beneath her hand. Rose shrugged, realising that somehow Silver Skin had magically transferred the qualities of the branch to the sword. She returned to her spot and her stance and watched as the tall youth approached her, his scimitar held before him in a high guard.

From where they watched the two combatants, Kye and Silver Skin held a conversation in their own tongue. If anyone other than Eloo listened they would have heard a number of grunts, whines and growls, for they were talking in the wolf tongue.

"Grer, what does Bright Eyes say about the sister?"

"Whine! It is as you feared, Kye. At her father's funeral she was seen in the company of the Black Queen and comforted by the Red Rook."

"Growl, then she is already lost."

"What do we, huff, tell her?"

"Whine! For the moment, nothing. She does not entirely trust us yet, she may not believe."

"Huff! But we must tell her something, grer, and soon."

"Huff! Is Moonstone looking into the, whine, prophecies?"

"Whine! Yes, she has been told and is, whine, looking into it."

"Huff! Then we wait until she tells us what she has, grer, found."

"Whine! Very well Kye, huff, but I do not like it."

"Whine! Neither do I, but I can see no other choice."

"Grer! Very well Kye, but there is a condition."

"Whine! Which is?"

"Whatever Moonstone finds we tell her what we know about her sister."

"Huff. Agreed, if she survives the Fire Drake."

"Whine. If any of us does, you mean."

Kye did not respond in either the common or wolf tongues, but gave Silver a deep growl which told Silver he agreed with her, but would not let that event happen while there was breath in his body.

A sentiment she agreed with by nodding.

FIRE AND ICE

"Extremis is the crucible of transformation."
The Book of the Wolf.

Rose was expecting him to strike at her sword hand, but with lightning quickness he changed stance and a flurry of quick blows rained down on her shield. Rose was rocked back on her heels by the force of the attack. She knew if she did not counter his attack would get past her guard, so she lunged at his stomach, but he was no longer there. He had leapt aside when she lunged, his blade flicking out at her side which she had opened to him as she extended her blade. His blade might have got her, but with the experience of both the dance master and the training ground, Rose darted away from his attack and spinning, blocked his attack with her own blade, which she managed to twist under his so that its tip was aimed at his throat.

"Yield?"

"Look down," he replied, in a deep but surprisingly musical voice.

Rose did, to find a dagger touching her stomach. She stepped back, releasing her blade and bringing it up to salute her combatant.

A look of surprise flashed in his eyes, and then he smiled as he matched her gesture.

"All right, I think that is enough to prove she can hold her own," Lightning said from where he was watching, his hands clasped behind his back.

"Has she, though?" Eloo said, a mischievous look on her face.

"She has proved she can dance with Lea, but can she avoid a Fire Dragon's breath?"

"What do you have in mind?" Silver Skin asked, a look of curiosity on her face.

"Fireball," Eloo said, her grin widening.

"Now just a minute—," Rose began.

"Eloo!" Lightning interjected, a look of worry crossing his face.

"Rose, Lightning, relax," Kye broke in, a look of annoyance aimed at Eloo. "Fire magic does not work within the hall, as she very well knows."

"It does raise a point," Silver Skin said, giving Rose a speculative look.

"What point?"

"That you are not fire proof," Silver Skin said, looking from Eloo to Lightning.

"We can protect her from fire," Eloo said.

"Besides which, we may not even need to fight," Lightning said, his confidence seeming to fall on deaf ears, as the rest of the party looked doubtful.

"Let us move," Kye said, his eyes moving to where the stone had been carved into a sundial. "We have lost enough time as it is, and I would like to be at the tomb of the heroes before nightfall."

With this he turned to the south and began to stride along the river bank, Lea and Lor falling into flanking position on his left and right and a little behind. Eloo and Silver were behind them and Rose found herself with Lightning at the rear.

"Where are we going?"

"The Tomb of the Heroes," Lightning said, as they hiked after the rest, Kye setting a fast march.

"And what is that?"

Striding out to keep up, Rose wondered how Eloo would keep up with the rest of the party who all had longer legs than her, but she saw to her amazement that Eloo hardly seemed to touch the ground as she bounded along at Silver's side. The taller woman's long strides never outpaced the smaller elf. Her attention went back to Lightning as he answered her question.

"The Tomb of the Heroes, or the Citadel, is a tomb where the three heroes from the mutant wars are buried."

This brought Rose up with a start. The mutant wars were the legendary and catastrophic events that brought about the end of the old world and began the dark ages that existed before her world came about. Rose had heard of the myth of such a time, but never imagined she might see some proof.

"Rose, is anything wrong?" Lightning asked, reminding her that the others were still moving and they were falling behind.

"No, it's just I heard of the mutant wars, but I know nothing about any heroes from that time. Who were they?"

"I know, but you would be better to ask Kye or even Lea, he is a bard after all. But come, we are falling behind."

Rose nodded, noting Lightning said Lea was a bard, one of the Druid orders she had heard about. They were recorders of histories and spoken histories, handed down from one mouth to another, or at least that was what she had heard.

They carried on along the river bank for another hour, at which point the river bent away from them and the forest reached out before them in a dense wall of trunks. Kye allowed a halt here, which Rose was grateful for as she was still out of shape from her injury. Though her shoulder was healed, she had not returned to full health and was finding it hard going.

"How much further?"

"About another half hour," Lightning said, his green eyes seeming to probe her. "How are you bearing up?"

"Fine," Rose lied, though her heavy breathing made the lie weightless.

Lightning grinned at her as if he believed her and with a twinkle in his eye, he turned to address Kye. "Kye, can we hang fire for a moment, I need a quick breather."

Kye turned from where he was examining a set of deer tracks on the edge of the wood. His yellow eyes fixed on the tall man and then swept over Rose, making her shiver, as she felt him probing her soul.

He might have disagreed, but Silver Skin interjected. "Kye, it might be a good time for us to hear how Fire Drakes like to fight if Lightning has the breath to tell us."

Kye snorted, shook his head and turned away to look at where an unkindness of ravens was picking over a kill.

"Well, Lightning, what can you tell us?"

"Silver, you are a Druidess. You probably know more than I do about Fire Drakes!"

"Maybe, but Rose and the others will not have heard, so perhaps you would oblige!"

Lightning sucked in his cheeks and cast an exaggerated look at the sky, a look making Rose giggle with delight. Then he became serious and began to lecture.

"If we are lucky, we may come on the Fire Drake unawares..."

Lightning was interrupted by a snort of disbelief from

Kye, who gave every indication of not paying attention as he watched the birds.

"As I was saying! We may come on him unawares, but this is unlikely as all dragons have senses better than most creatures. Still, it is always a possibility..."

"Not a probability," muttered Kye.

"If he does detect us, he is likely to attack."

"Is that certain?" Lea asked in his deep musical voice.

"I suppose he might parley," Lightning said, a speculative look creeping over his face. "But he is more likely to attack and ask questions later. If..."

"When," Kye said impatiently.

"When or if he attacks, it is best to avoid his fire so I would suggest we stay far apart to make his number of targets as many as possible."

Rose was possessed by the image of a great bird like lizard flying above her, a tongue of fire licking at her.

"Unfortunately, that may also help the drake," Silver said, softly.

"How?"

"Because, Rose, the dragon's goal is to divide and conquer. As a group we may be enough to beat him, but as individuals we are just fodder," Lightning said.

"That sounds great."

"Don't worry," Lightning said, his usual grin returning. "Silver and Kye have dealt with drakes before and they know, as I do, ways to get round him."

Rose was about to ask what ways when Eloo broke in. "Kye, what is it?"

Turning to look at the tall werewolf, Rose noted he was rigid. His yellow eyes fixed on the spot where the ravens were still picking over the bones of whatever it was. However, by his vacant stare she guessed he was not seeing them.

"What's wrong with him?"

"He's in the grip of a vision," Silver Skin said, her own eyes scouring the same spot as Kye, but she seemed to find nothing, or at least she did not see what Kye was seeing.

Eloo flew to his side, but did not, as Rose expected, grab Kye and shake him, but instead gently touched his arm, asking in a barely audible voice, "Kye, can you hear me?"

For a long time he did not respond and when they had all given up hope, his hoarse voice croaked a response. "The spirits are calling to me."

"What do they say?" Silver asked, her eyes sweeping the spot, but still she found nothing.

"The Citadel is under attack."

"The Fire Drake?"

"I cannot see, but it is under attack. I can see Heather, she says her tomb is disturbed..."

Rose realised once again Kye had referred to someone called Heather, and his voice sounded as though her name gave him pain.

"Does she say anything more?"

Kye did not respond for a long time and then he shook his head as though clearing it. When he turned his eyes on Eloo, they were no longer far away, but intense with purpose. "We must get there now!"

"But it's another half hour..."

"Not as the wolf runs," Kye barked.

"But you cannot go on your own," Eloo said, desperately. "You cannot take on the Fire Drake on your own."

"He won't be alone," cut in Lor. His voice was gravelly and gave Rose the idea of bark grating on bark.

"No," Silver said, her voice a bark of command. Her voice resonated with so much power even Rose felt it vibrate in her mind.

Rose watched as Silver Skin's words made all the other werewolves draw up to attention, as though Silver was their commander. Even Kye, who glared daggers at Silver, felt her authority and though he growled, he nodded his acceptance.

"Then let's go, if we're going," he growled. Turning, he jogged into the trees, his pace now all but running.

Rose would have liked to ask Lightning or Silver a ton of questions, like who Heather had been and what the Citadel was, but the pace Kye was setting was too fast and she only had breath to run.

She was almost dropping when Lightning, who had never left her side, handed her a small silver mounted leather flask.

"Drink this, it will give you strength."

Rose expected to wince as she uncapped the flask, but she was not, as she expected, embraced by a strong smell of liquor. The smell was strong, but it was sweet and flowery like the perfume of a flower smelt in the darkness of a hot summer night.

"What is it?"

"Fire Blossom it's called, it's a brew of my own. Don't worry, it will give you vigour."

Rose stared into his dark green eyes, dancing with humour, and found herself lifting it to her lips. What surprised her, was not that she was doing so, but that she trusted him enough to do so. Her father had taught her about poisons and warned her to never taste something no one else had tasted first, but here she was about to drink. She tried to analyse why and there was only one explanation, she trusted him! She could not explain why, she did not even know herself. She only knew she did trust this man implicitly, even though she had only met him the night before.

She sipped the thick liquid and although she spluttered as it caught the back of her throat, it quickly turned to a warm glow spreading to every corner of her being. As Lightning had promised, she felt energised and stronger, as if she could go for the rest of the day without a rest.

"Rose, if that's one of Lightning's brews pass it around," Eloo said, bounding past.

Rose passed it back to Lightning, who after taking a deep draw handed it to Silver who passed it on. The drink fortified her and she did not feel any effects of the quick march until they stopped. Then she felt her muscles give a dull ache that she guessed would kill her the next day, but for now she revelled in this proof of her being alive. Still, this feeling soon disappeared as she became aware of her surroundings.

The trees had thinned to reveal a large lake lying across their path. However, although the lake was imposing enough in its size, it was what was reflected in the waters that really impressed itself upon her mind. Across from them was a towering structure made of dark grey stone that must have been several storeys tall.

"Is that the Citadel?"

"Yes," Kye said, his yellow eyes fixed on the grey monolith.

"But it looks untouched," Rose said, thinking that it also looked untouchable.

Kye opened his mouth to respond, but stopped, a hand raised, as the relative quiet was broken by a loud voice echoing round the clearing. Its deep tone bouncing back from the water, trees and stone as they intoned words in a strange language.

"In nomine spiritum of Terra I ordo you aperire!"

Kye's eyes narrowed as the words faded away, leaving a greater silence than had existed before their sounding.

"That was an unbinding spell," Lightning said in a hoarse whisper.

Kye growled and began to string his bow. Eloo hesitantly put a hand on his arm.

"Kye I know you want to get in there, but remember it might be the Fire Drake, and you may need ice arrows."

"Is there time?" Lor asked.

Another stream of words broke out across the clearing. Rose shivered as their strange hissing tone slivered their way into her ears.

"He is trying to breach the wards," Silver Skin said, her head cocked. "He must not be able to breach the defences."

Kye glanced at the sky and muttered something about needing the moon.

"It is full," Silver said. "Her power maybe strong enough to achieve the spell."

Kye grunted and knelt among the reeds at the water's edge. Rose could not see him well, so she moved up beside him. He had extracted from the arrow bag at his waist three feathered shafts. Rose first took them for normal arrows, but on a closer inspection she saw they had no heads, but were blunt shafts. As Rose watched, he dipped the shafts into the water, and clutching the silver chain around his neck, began to chant in a strange language. Rose realised that once again she was seeing magic performed. Somehow, though she did not know how she knew it, she could tell this magic was different to the spell Silver had used earlier to change the sword and was different to that being shouted by the invisible person.

As Rose watched the water around the arrow tips go cloudy she felt the air near Kye drop in temperature, as if Kye's words were leaching heat out of the air to power his spell. When Kye pulled the shafts back out of the water the arrows had heads of a glowing blue that did not look like metal, so much as ice. The arrows now appeared to be feathered icicles. Kye passed one to Lor and one to Lea and nocked the last one to his now strung war bow. There was another thing Rose could now see and that was what was hanging around Kye's neck. From a narrow chain of silver, there hung a medallion crafted to resemble a disk that was three quarters silver and a quarter black metal. The symbol made her think of a three quarter moon.

Meanwhile, Silver, too, had been grasping her medallion and casting magic.

"Come here, each of you," she said, and held out her hands to them.

Rose saw Silver was holding in one hand a phial of liquid that must be very cold, as ice crystals had formed down one side of the glass. Each of the party stepped forwards and allowed Silver to touch them. All three of the werewolves knelt and bowed their heads, as if they were receiving a blessing. Then it was Rose's turn and she gazed into Silver's eyes, searching them, for what? She had always been told magic was evil and should never be used, under any circumstances. But here she was, allowing a woman she only met that morning cast some spell on her, why? Why wasn't she running or stopping Silver? Perhaps because, in her heart of hearts, she knew Silver was not evil.

As if sensing her reluctance, Silver spoke softly. "This spell will give you some protection from the Fire Dragon's fiery breath."

Rose realised she believed her, and closing her eyes nodded to Silver who touched her on the brow. As she did, Rose felt a slight chill pass from her touch through her blood. It felt as if ice-water was running through her veins, but almost as soon as the feeling had come it was gone and Rose felt normal. She heard a slight crack and when she opened her eyes, she found Silver was now clutching a broken phial. Rose realised Lightning had not been touched by Silver.

"What about Lightning? He won't be protected."

"Thank you for worrying about me, Rose," Lightning said, smiling at her. "But I am a fire caster. I have an innate protection from fire. The dragon's breath will have no effect on me. The werewolves are, however, beings of water, isn't that right, Kye?"

Kye did not answer, but pointed to Lea and Lor and indicated the left hand side of the lake. They nodded and turned around, disappearing in the direction they had just come from. Then he and Eloo began to drift along the shore line.

"Where did the twins go?"

"Shush," Silver whispered.

Rose looked from her to Lightning and he moved closer to whisper in her ear, a sensation she found she liked.

"We must be as quiet as we can, Rose. Fire Drakes have excellent senses. To answer your question, the twins are making a larger circle through the trees, while Kye and Eloo move closer. We approach from the other side of the lake." As Lightning said this, he handed Rose a crossbow and drew from his belt a slender wand. "Can you use it?" he asked, pointing at the crossbow.

Rose nodded, and placing the bow's stock against her shoulder she followed Silver and Lightning as they strode along the lake's shore.

The lake was not as large as Rose thought. In minutes they had moved round the top of the lake and through a copse of willow and were approaching the building from the other side. As they rounded the corner of the stone structure, they came in view of the clearing in front of the building. Rose glanced at a pair of stone doors, set in an arch, but what caught and held her attention was the tall, black robed figure standing before the doors. Rose was taken aback by this hooded figure for it looked like a man, not the huge lizard she had been expecting.

"It's a man," she exclaimed and would have asked one of her companions, but Silver hushed her.

The hood began to turn in their direction when Eloo stepped out of the trees behind him and pointed her rod at his robed back.

"In the name of the Sylvan Throne, I order you to explain your presence here."

The figure spun round to face Eloo. Seeing her standing there aiming her wand at him, he snarled something and to Rose's amazement he shot up into the air as though a rocket had been lit under him. Eloo cried something and there was a flash of light that left Rose blinded. She was for a moment afraid she was permanently blinded, but Lightning's voice came to her, through the veil of darkness.

"It's okay, Rose, your sight will clear in a moment."

She blinked and found he was right. After a few moments, her vision cleared to reveal Eloo pointing her rod up at the sky, which had darkened, as if a storm had sprung up from nowhere. Following

Eloo's gaze and pointing wand, Rose gazed up to see a sight that both amazed and shocked her, her mouth falling open as she stared.

The sun had gone out because hanging above them like a thunder cloud was the huge form of the Fire Drake. Rose had expected a winged lizard, but the reality was a thousand times more impressive. The creature was huge. Rose had once seen the preserved remains of a creature from the old world called an elephant, that was until now the largest creature she had ever seen, but the drake was much larger than that ancient beast. It filled the sky like a thunder cloud, though it was red and not black. The beast was bright scarlet, burning in the sky like a new sun. The dragon, however, was not flying above them, but hovering like a cloud. Its massive wings, the colour of smoke, were spread out to either side of the creature, but were not moving. The beast hung there, as if buoyed up by invisible winds. When it spoke its voice was like thunder, deep and rumbling, and it filled the woods with its depth and power.

"Who dares to attack me?"

From beside her, Rose heard Lightning speak. "Great Fire Lord, we represent the Sylvan Throne, who would ask why you are burning so widely."

The cloud of a dragon tilted its head slightly, as if finding Lightning, but its attention returned to Eloo below it.

"The Throne would prevent me from following my nature?"

"No, but they might ask you to be less damaging and they ask you to return to your slumbers."

This apparently did not please the dragon, for it let loose a roar that shook the trees and vibrated through Rose's boots. As if this was a signal, several things happened at once. Eloo unleashed a bolt of energy from her wand, two arrows flew out of the trees and the dragon unleashed a gout of fire. Rose had expected the fire to be impressive, but she was shocked by its power and heat. She was fifty feet below the dragon, but she could feel the heat even from this distance. As Rose got over the shock of the fire she realised the trees that were now ablaze held not only Kye, but also Lea and Lor.

"Lightning, the others are in there!"

This idea must have occurred to Eloo too, for she unleashed a terrible cry more like the roar of some great cat than a woman.

When Rose glanced at her, she seemed larger than before, as

though she had swelled with rage. Her eyes were no longer green, but black like thunder clouds, and her long hair was streaming out behind her in a high wind that had sprung up from nowhere. Tiny bolts of lightning crackled and flared around her and as Rose watched she began to rise into the air. Rose saw her rod's flower bud-like tip was opening, to fold out into individual petals that slid back to form a barbed and pointed end, which began to glow with red light as if a bolt of lightning was building up at its tip. The tip trembled as Eloo lost control of her emotions.

The dragon, who had been watching her like a cat watching a mouse, began to chant in his strange language. Rose guessed from the feeling of energy thickening the air that the dragon was casting a spell. Her father, who she had always suspected knew more than he should about magic, had told her if she ever came up against a magic user the best way to protect herself was to distract them and interrupt their casting. Aiming her crossbow at the glittering belly she fired at it. Simultaneously, Eloo let loose another scream of rage and the glowing point of her wand discharged a brilliant bolt of energy. Almost at the same time, one of the ice headed arrows flew out of the trees to strike the dragon's smoky wing. Rose watched in amazement as the wing turned from smoke into ice. Ice began to spread out in waves of crystals that quickly spread to freeze the wing.

The dragon roared again, and to Rose's shock and amazement it burst into flames. Suddenly the red thunder cloud turned into a new sun, burning away all the shadows. Rose shielded her eyes against the red glow, to see the dragon's body covered in a nimbus of dancing flames. At first, Rose wondered if Eloo's bolt had done this, but Lightning's voice murmured in her ear, denying this.

"He has surrounded his body in fire."

Rose was about to ask what they should do next, when a huge drop of water struck her arm. Rose realised that beyond the glowing dragon and the burning trees, the sky was black. As this idea sank in, the heavens opened and the trees, the dragon and everything else was drenched in water. This enraged the dragon even more, and with another roar it beat its wings, sending a torrent of scalding water down on its attackers. Rose might have been bathed in scalding water, but Lightning, seeing what would happen dragged her out of the way with one hand and unleashed a stream of sonic energy in the dragon's direction with the other. The burst he unleashed, screamed through the air like a banshee's wail and hurt Rose's ears but if it hit the dragon she did not see it, for it was now veiled in a cloud of white steam. For a moment the clearing was still, save for the hissing of steam. Even Lea and Lor's arrowfire stopped for they could no longer see the dragon through its cloak of steam. Then it burst out of the cloud to swoop down at Eloo.

Lightning, seeing the dragon's goal, fired another screaming burst at it, but the burst broke like water against the rock of the dragon's hide as he grabbed hold of Eloo with a massive forepaw. The shriek of the sonic burst had only just faded away when the clearing was filled by another howl, this one that of a wolf, and Kye's huge black form leapt from the smoking wood to launch itself at the dragon. The dragon turned its head in Kye's direction and unleashed a second stream of fire at him, but Kye was too quick. Before the dragon could hit him with its breath or fly off he had sprung upon the dragon's wing and was biting and clawing at it. Rose winced to see this, for although the dragon's nimbus of fire had disappeared its skin was still red hot, steam rising around it. But Kye gave no sign of noticing as he tore at the wing the dragon beat in an attempt to dislodge the wolf.

From the woods Lea and Lor emerged to fire a storm of arrows at the dragon, while from by Lightning's side, Silver used her staff to fire a ray of blue light that transformed the steaming water into a sheaf of ice wherever it touched. The dragon roared as Eloo, still held in its claw, continued to blast it with electricity from her rod. Finally, the dragon gave such a heave with its wing it sent Kye flying, and quick as a striking snake it twisted round to unleash a burst of fiery breath on the werewolf. Rose, seeing this, realised though Silver and Lea were moving to help him, none of them would reach him before the dragon unleashed its destructive breath. Before she realised what she was doing, she was rushing towards the dragon, her shield held up before her, her sword in a protective stance.

She reached the wolf to find him trying to get to his huge feet. But from the way he was groggily shaking his massive head she could tell he was too dazed to avoid the dragon's attack. So stepping past his huge form, she moved towards the monster and as she did so she took in the head of the beast before her.

She had imagined the dragon's head would resemble a lizard or scaly cat, sleek and deadly, but the horn crowned death's head glaring at her was a skull with no snout, but simple nose holes. As she watched, its underhung jaw dropped like a many spiked drawbridge to reveal the glowing furnace of its throat. She lifted her gaze to meet the dragon's glowing red eyes. Seeing in their fiery reflection her own frightened face she knew she was about to die. Even as this realisation hit her the dragon opened its jaws wide and Rose could see the dazzling glare of its inner fires. Then the wall of fire was racing towards her.

Rose heard the roar of the flames as they whooshed towards her, but to her amazement she felt cool and calm as she faced her death. What startled her more, was over the roar of the approaching fire she heard her voice calmly speaking. She did not understand the words she was saying, but she knew it was her voice.

"Praesidum Ego from nocere."

Rose did not understand the words, but she recognised the language in which she had said them. She had just spoken in the magical tongue the dragon had used. How was that possible when she knew nothing about magic? Despite her shock, Rose could not move from the approaching fire. She watched as it approached, but as it did saw the glow of the fire had grown dimmer. As the fire reached her, it hit an invisible barrier which blocked the flames and shielded Rose from the heat. Watching from behind a tinted barrier she saw the flames sweeping around her. The fire moved on, leaving her behind and untouched by the heat which would have killed her.

As she realised this, she also realised the fire had passed her by to reach Kye.

AN UNDERSTANDING OF MAGIC

"Magic is more than just words and gestures. It has a life of its own and the results are not always what you expect of them."
Takana the Harpy, the Wereding chronicles.

Silver watched as the fire shot from between the dragon's jaws and towards Rose, who she was powerless to protect, and her jaw dropped when she heard Rose pronounce the words of power that protected her from the dragon's breath. This meant she was all but oblivious to the swiftly approaching wash of flames. It was Kye who saved her life, by knocking her legs out from under her so that she fell across his neck and shoulders. Then he was pounding for the trees, his swift strides carrying them out of the path of the fire.

"No, Kye, stop, we must end this now."

The wolf stopped, and spinning on the spot let Silver slip off him, before he went charging back at the dragon, who was snarling in frustration at Rose, who to Silver's pleasure, fear and amazement had just struck the monster on its jaw with her sword. The dragon responded by snapping its jaw at her in an attempt to bite her. Rose, however, stepped back, taking her out of range of the beast's jaw, which was fortunate, for she suddenly sank to her knees, her head falling forward, as if she was a puppet that had just had its strings cut. Silver had not seen Rose receive a wound, nor had the dragon been casting. She hoped Rose had succumbed to the strength sapping side effects of magic use. This weakening of its attacker had not gone unnoticed by the dragon, who tasted the air with its unbelievably long tongue. A tongue which flickered with flames. It might have done more, but at that moment Kye came snarling at it and the dragon was forced to turn its attention to him.

The beast half turned towards Kye, and swinging a mace-like tail swept him off his feet and tumbling head over heels. Kye tried to leap back to the attack, but the Fire Drake was not about to let him and followed the tail sweep up with a second blow, one that impacted with a bone crunching force which tore a painful whimper from Kye.

This sound seemed to be the last thing holding Eloo back and the inhuman scream torn from her was followed by a tornado of wind that came from nowhere to drive rain, sleet and lightning straight into the dragon's face.

Silver grinned grimly. Eloo was giving her the diversion she needed. As Eloo raised Cain, the dragon roared and tried to lift itself off the ground with its damaged wings. Silver guessed it was trying to make its escape but she was not about to let that happen. Planting her staff in the ground, she gathered her strength and began to cast.

Rose could not understand why she felt so weak, but she did. Her legs folded beneath her and her vision blurred with fatigue. She was dimly aware of Kye's charge and his howl of pain, but she could only take it in with part of her mind. The other part was telling her to sleep. She was grateful when Eloo's storm passed over her on its way to strike the dragon, for the cold sleet of the storm was like a slap in the face. It did not remove the fatigue entirely, but it was the shock she needed to come back to the world around her. Then Lightning was crouching beside her, his large eyes staring at her with naked concern in them.

"Are you all right, Rose?" he asked, firing his crossbow in the dragon's direction, but his aim was very wide.

"Tired."

"It's the strain of spell casting," he explained, repeatedly and pointlessly pulling the bow's trigger. "It'll wear off in a minute."

Rose was about to say she didn't do spells, when a roar from the dragon made her look back in its direction. The dragon's head was now crusted in ice and one of its eyes swollen shut, but it was still on its feet and its anger was concentrated on Eloo. Its tail arched up over its back like a Scorpion's and indeed its bladed and spiked club of a tail was lengthening into a stinger meant to arch over and strike Eloo.

Kye had other ideas. Even as the sting quivered for the strike, Kye leapt onto its back. His jaws closed on its poisonous tip and sliced it off. The dragon roared with rage and with a spasmodic arching of its back flung Kye into the air, and Eloo's limp body dropped from its claw. The creature rose several feet into the air without flapping its wings and from there tried to fly away, its damaged wings struggling to move it through the air.

It turned towards the tomb, as if to fly north, but it found an unexpected obstacle in that direction. The sky was full of black thunderheads which roiled and swirled like a disturbed cauldron, their innards lit by flashes of light that did not appear to be normal lightning. It was as though the lake itself had risen up to block the dragon's escape. It wheeled to face south, but found its path blocked by a picket line of the twins, Silver Skin and Kye in his human form, his bow stretched to full draw. The dragon roared in anger as Silver began to chant. Kye loosed his bow, almost at the same instant as the dragon let loose its killing breath. Rose blinked, trying to see past the brightness of the red glow, but when the glare died she saw the four werewolves stood there untouched by the fire, though the ground around them was scorched and burnt.

"Silver's magic protected them," Lightning muttered in her ear.

"But the dragon, where is he?"

"Making good his escape."

Rose followed Lightning's pointing hand, to see above the smoking tree line a dark spot against the blue sky.

"He's got away?"

"Not for long," Silver said, leaning on her staff. "The pack is tracking him. They will make sure he does no more damage."

Rose was about to ask what would happen when a flash of light at the edge of her eye stopped her. Turning, she saw a glowing green orb floating about six feet off the ground.

"One of the tomb's guardian spirits," Silver Skin gasped.

Rose watched with surprise as Kye dropped to his knees and held out his hands.

"Heather!" Kye breathed.

The orb may or may not have been Heather, but it responded to the name as it flew through the air to hover inches before Kye's face. Kye reached out slowly and very gently touched the orb, which reacted by changing colour, as ripples of dark shades flickered across the orb. Kye rocked back on his heels and the orb shot away from him, rocketing into the sky to disappear into the fading storm over the lake. Rose turned from the shredding clouds to see, with surprise, tears flowing down Kye's face.

"Kye, are you hurt?" Lightning asked.

"Not physically," he whispered, wiping the tears from his eyes with his long hair.

"What did it tell you?"

"Lightning!" Lor objected. "What a spirit tells you is private."

"Your pardon."

"It is all right, Lor," Kye said, his hard mask now in place. "What Heather said to me is for you all."

"Then it was Heather?"

"Yes, Silver, it was," Kye said, a tinge of the pained expression flickering across his face to disappear again. "But come, Eloo should hear this too."

It was only then Rose realised Eloo was not standing with them.

"Where is she? Is she all right?"

Rose wasn't sure, but she thought she saw the flicker of a smile touch Kye's lips.

"She is among the trees, resting and recovering."

"Recovering?"

"The use of magic, if abused or over used can drain the wielder of strength," Lightning explained, as they moved towards the tree line. "That is why you feel so fatigued. You cast a spell and it drained you."

Rose stopped and stared at Lightning as she tried to accept what she had just heard.

"But I didn't cast a spell. I have never cast magic."

"I am afraid I must disagree."

"But I haven't... I don't understand this..."

"We shall talk about it shortly, but now Kye is waiting."

Rose found Eloo lying on a bed of cloaks among unburnt leaf litter just inside the tree line, her curtain of black hair spread out beneath her. Its darkness emphasised the pallor of her usually dark skin.

"Is she all right?"

Kye dropped down to her side and placed a hand on her forehead.

Eloo, who had been lying with her eyes closed, opened her luminous green orbs and stared up into Kye's face. What she saw there made her smile wanly. "It's okay, Kye, I just need to rest."

"She's going to be fine," Lightning whispered to Rose.

"Kye," Silver said, softly drawing him from Eloo and reminding him that they were there too. "What did Heather tell you?"

"Heather? Heather was here?" Eloo asked, half rising on one elbow, a mix of emotions crossing her feline features.

"She has left again," Kye said, easing her back down. "But before she left, she spoke to me. She said the Fire Drake was trying to get into the Citadel."

"But we already know that," Lea said.

"But she told us more," Kye said calmly, though his eyes never left Eloo's. "She told us he was after the Wand of Wisdom."

"So that is what happened to it," Lightning said, sharing a look with Silver.

"But what would a Fire Drake want with such an artefact?"

"What is this wand?" Rose asked, before she could stop herself. "Or is that a question I shouldn't ask?"

"No question should not be asked, Rose," Silver said, a gentle smile tugging at her lips. "However, the question may not be answered. Still, never hesitate to ask a question, no one here will think the worse of you for it. The Wand is a magical artefact used in The Mutant Wars, to bolster the magic of the forces of good. It was said to be a great source of magical power, but it disappeared not long after the wars."

"But none of this explains why the drake was after it."

"Dragons sometimes wield enormous power to obtain their goals."

"Perhaps," Lightning agreed, though he looked sceptical.

"Lightning, what do you think?"

"If he wanted to take over another's lair or a kingdom maybe..."

"But you don't think so." Silver's words were a statement, not a question.

"Dragon Games," Lea muttered.

"What's that?" Rose asked.

"Blood and flames are the result when dragons play their games," Lea said, giving a significant glance at Lightning.

"Unfair, unfair," Lightning said, meeting Lea's gaze.

Rose felt she was hearing part of a long and on-going argument between the two. However, Lor did not give her the chance to ask what they were talking about.

"Will he return?"

"Not for a long time," Lightning said, after a long period of consideration. "He will need time to recover from his attack and anyway, drakes never do anything twice."

"But he may send someone else to do it for him," Lor pointed out. "Does that mean we need to retrieve it?"

"It is in the citadel and therefore a Druid matter," Silver said, an air of gravity entering her voice.

"But you are a Druid," Lor pointed out. "Kye is an Ovate and Lea is a Bard. We can call a Triad."

Rose watched as the three werewolves exchanged looks. As she did, she could not but help feel that a private and possibly telepathic conversation was being exchanged. After a long moment Kye nodded and Silver turned her back on the group. She drew in a long breath and spoke to them, but did not look at anyone.

"Lor, find me a deer or weasel to kill. Rose, Lightning, make a fire. It will be dark soon and I need light to work."

"You could use cold light," Lor suggested.

"I will need all my strength for the rites. We will have to make do with ordinary firelight."

Lightning turned to Rose and grinned cheekily. "So, how would you like to come fire hunting?"

Rose, grinning back, pretended to think about the offer and then nodded. They moved off deeper into the trees, gathering up fallen branches and leaves. As they did, Rose decided to ask some of the questions which were burning her brain.

"Lightning, can I ask you what just happened?"

"What, you mean Lor's little clanger?"

"Clanger?"

"Haven't you heard that one before?"

"As it happens, no. Go on, anyway."

"Well, I shouldn't tell you, but since Lor has let the cat out of the bag anyway. The Druid order is made up of three orders..."

"The Druids, the bards and ovate, I knew that."

"My dear Rose, everyone knows that," Lightning said, and although Rose could not see his face in the glooming, she could tell from his voice he was grinning. "But what you and most people do not know, is if a Druid, Bard and Ovate are present they can speak for the order and make decisions and judgements that can affect the whole of the order and probably the rest of the Wereding world."

"So, what is going to happen?"

"Silver will perform a ritual that will call spirits to come and help the Druid Triad make their decisions. Then the three will debate and judge on what they wish to decide."

"Spirits. Then that globe was the soul of a dead person?"

"Yes, Heather's soul to be precise."

"And who is or was Heather?"

"Heather was Kye's mate many years ago, I believe."

"Then Eloo is not his lover?"

"Of course she is, but Eloo was not always Kye's mate. Heather was before her and then she died or was killed. I am not sure about the details. As you might have noted it is not easy getting blood out of that particular stone."

"You don't say?"

"Any other brilliant observations?"

"Actually, I do have another question for you."

"What, just one?"

"Back there you said I used magic, but I have never had anything to do with magic. So how is that possible?"

"I don't know, Rose, but what I do know is you spoke in the old tongue and you cast a protective spell. You asked the magic to protect you and it did. It shielded you from the fire."

"You speak as if the magic is alive."

"Who says it isn't? More often than not we call on the magic to help us and it has unexpected effects and does things we didn't expect it to. As to you not knowing any magic or magic words, I do not know what to tell you..."

"Is there anyone who might?" Rose asked, as they moved back towards the tomb and its clearing.

"We could ask Silver. There is much the Druids know about magic, or we could ask Takana."

"And who is that?"

"My master, well mistress. She is the teacher at the fire school."

"And what do you learn there?"

"About fire magic, and if you're very good, I might even show you some."

When they got back to the clearing it was to find Silver, Kye and Lea all sitting cross legged in front of the stone structure. They appeared to be meditating on the house of death. At least, they were facing it, with lowered heads and closed eyes.

"Should we disturb them?"

Before Lightning could respond the three figures sprang to life, as though they had been some of the windup mechanoids Rose had seen at fairs. One moment they were as still as death, the next they were erect, their eyes gleaming out of the half-light.

"Where do you want the wood put?" Lightning said, not affected by this change.

For a long time Silver did not answer him, just fixing him with that searching gaze these werewolves seemed to unleash at will. After an age Silver answered in a voice falling as soft as rain. "Here, in the centre of the clearing."

Rose watched as Lightning dropped his load of firewood and knelt to arrange it. After a while she, too, laid the wood next to his pile, watching the three druids out of the corner of her eye.

"Do you want it lit yet?"

Silver turned to Kye and they shared a look, which he answered with a nod.

"Yes, please, Lightning."

"Rose, you are lucky, you are about to see some fire magic after all."

Rose watched closely as Lightning began to make gestures over the nest of wood. His hands made passes over the wood pile and as he weaved in the air he chanted under his breath. Rose could not make out what Lightning was saying, he could have been playing around, but she could feel the build of magic in the air. There was a feeling of the air thickening and she tasted copper and could smell a whiff of electricity in the air, as though a thunderstorm was gathering.

For a moment nothing happened and then smoke began to curl up from the wood and a flame sprang up and the wood was suddenly crackling. As the fire flared up, it cast the three figures' shadows long and large against the stone walls of the tomb. Rose shuddered, feeling the power which was now gathered within these figures. It was as though with the lighting of this fire, the three figures had become giants, imbued with power beyond Rose's comprehension.

Rose turned away from the tomb and its shadows and studied Lightning. He seemed tall, but she felt he was not intimidating. In fact, she felt he was someone to whom she could turn, a shoulder to cry on.

"What now?" she whispered to Lightning.

"Lor will bring something to be sacrificed." The voice which answered Rose was not Lightning's, but Eloo's, and it came from beside them.

THE SUMMONING OF SPIRITS

"The Druid lives in two worlds and is a physical bridge between the world of the material and the world of the spirits. When they need guidance, they look beyond the veil."
Bright Eyes, from the Wereding chronicles by the Red Wizard.

Rose turned to find Eloo standing beside them, her ghostly whiteness gone, her eyes glowing with emerald fires.

"What kind of sacrifice?"

"That kind."

Rose turned to look where she was pointing, to see Lor leading a young deer by a noose. As Rose watched the young animal moving skittishly into the firelight she saw its soft dove eyes blink at her. As they touched eyes, Rose could feel the spirit of the animal gaze back at her and her heart lurched.

"You're going to kill it?"

"That's why they call it a sacrifice."

"But you can't," Rose said, and she could hear tears in her voice.

"Why not?" Eloo asked, seeming totally confused. "You've eaten venison before, haven't you?"

"It's all for the greater good, Rose," Lightning said, sensing her agitation. "If the powers did not want this, Lor could not have trapped it."

"How do you figure that?"

"Silence," came Silver's voice, and it was no longer like rain, but like the winter's frost, cold and biting. If Rose would have tried to protest before, she felt all will to do so freeze solid in her, at the power and command of this voice.

She turned towards the triad, to find Lea holding a set of pipes, Kye clutching a bowl and Silver a long bladed knife. She watched as Lor drew near to the three, but did not yet bring the young deer to them. Silver raised her arms to the sky and began to chant, as Lea played his flute. Rose did not understand the words of Silver's chant, as they were in a tongue she did not know, but as the chant went on words she knew entered her mind without travelling through her ears.

"In the Silver Goddesses name, we invoke you."

"What is she doing?"

"Silver is summoning the spirits, to help with the rite."

"Shush," Eloo hissed, her green eyes glowing in the firelight as she watched Kye.

Rose studied the tall werewolf who was staring into the bowl, which appeared to be made of stone, its lip carved with strange runes and symbols.

With a gesture from Silver, Lor brought the deer forward and Kye held the bowl beneath the deer's throat, as Silver approached with the knife. Rose watched with amazement as the deer lifted its head, exposing its throat, as though willing to offer up its life without a fight. She stared in disbelief as the deer looked to the sky, as if searching for something in the heavens. As if it would give its soul to a deity as Silver drew her blade across the fawn's throat.

The blood did not explode out of the deer's throat like Rose expected it to. It flowed yes, but slowly, and Kye withdrew the bowl before the blood had stopped flowing, so it fell onto the ground, but instead of forming a bloody pool it disappeared, as though the ground drank the blood up. Lor drew the fawn to the fire and Lightning, using a metal tool, burnt the wound closed. Rose was aware of this and could smell the burning flesh, but she could not bring herself to look at the fawn. So she concentrated on the actions of the triad.

Silver turned to the tomb and held up the bloody knife in a gesture of presentation. Kye held up the bowl before his face. Staring into the mirror of blood inside, he too spoke in the strange tongue, and as he did, the strangest part of the rite so far happened.

As Kye intoned, the clearing became brighter. Rose, searching for the light, at first thought the moon had risen, but it was still hidden by clouds. So where was the light coming from? Then Rose saw the source of the light. It was orbs, like the green one that appeared to Kye earlier, but there were dozens of them and they were all colours.

As she watched they levitated towards the triad. The three figures were now surrounded by many colours that appeared to pour through the three rather than silhouette them, as though the three were lanterns. Rose became aware of many whispering voices, carried to her on the wind. She tried to listen to them but they were as ephemeral as the lights, which were fading fast. Suddenly the lights were gone and the fire was snuffed out by a strong wind. The clearing, however, was not dark for long, for even as Rose watched the moon came out from behind the clouds and flooded the clearing with its silver light.

The moon's bright light revealed the three werewolves were no longer facing the tomb, but were now facing Rose, their eyes fixed on her. She opened her mouth to ask them what they had seen or heard, but a streak of light distracted her. She saw a very small orb of blue light, floating away from the bowl in Kye's hands and gliding to where Lor held the fawn. Hearing a snuffling from that direction, Rose turned to see Lor releasing the fawn, which blinked at her and then trotted off in the direction of the lake.

"But Silver cut its throat!"

"And the Lady sent its spirit back," Lightning said, as he rekindled the fire with a flick of his wrist.

"But you knew this would happen, so why didn't you tell me?"

"Because the spirit is not always returned, sometimes the Lady keeps them," Lor said, and wrapped the noose around his waist.

"Never mind that," Lightning interrupted. "What did the spirits say?"

"First, tea," Eloo broke in. "Can't you see they need something hot in them? They are spent!"

Eloo was quite right, the three appeared tired and drained. Kye was bowed down, as though he was weighed by a great burden. Eloo flew to Kye's side and covered his face in kisses as she led him to the fire, where Lor had produced (as if by magic) a spit and kettle, boiling already.

"Kye, can you hear me?" Eloo asked quietly, staring at him, but he did not respond. His eyes were still fixed on Rose.

"Kye!" Eloo almost barked this at him and the concern in her voice broke through his daze. He met her eyes and nodded. Rose was glad she was no longer under that hard, penetrating gaze.

"Are you okay?" Eloo asked, caressing his face.

"Yes," Kye whispered, his voice cracked and hoarse. "Cold!"

"Get that down you," Lor said, forcing a tin mug into his hands.

Kye might have thanked Lor, Rose did not hear, for she was listening to what Silver was saying, in an equally hoarse voice.

"I knew Heather was there and perhaps Holly, I am not sure. But who was there is not as important as what they told us, Lor..."

"And what did they say about me?" It took a handful of heartbeats, for Rose to realise she had spoken.

Silver turned to face her, and Rose took an involuntary step back, for the woman's face had changed greatly. Not only was Silver Skin's face grey and lined, as if she had become an old woman, but the wolf inside her had become more striking. Her eyes were a glaring yellow, the pupils dark and dilated. The skin was drawn tight over her cheekbones making her long jaw seem even longer, and as she met Rose's glare, her top lip wrinkled in a snarl half unsheathing her fangs.

"What the spirits told us, may not concern you at all."

"Peace, Silver," Lea said softly, laying a hand on his older sister's shoulder. "Rose feels our gaze, she deserves to know what we may think about her part in the spirits' words."

Silver shrugged Lea's hand off her shoulder and took several deep breaths, which not only calmed her but removed some of the look of the wolf from her. When she spoke again, her voice was no longer a harsh growl.

"Forgive me, Rose. My anger is not at you, but at the mist before me." Rose was surprised as Silver cast her snarls aside and laughed. "I don't know why I am getting angry! It is the lot of my calling, to grope in dark riddles and mysteries."

"What mysteries?"

"The Rose will bleed for the land and her blood will start a miracle. A miracle that will either save or destroy the world. Only the red bird can decide its fate. These were the words of the spirits."

Kye's voice was low, but it dropped into the silence of the clearing like stones falling into a deep pool.

After a long time, Lightning broke the silence.

"Is this all they said?"

"No," Silver said. "They do not always speak in words, sometimes they show us things, but that can be as much a riddle as their words. Kye, you saw the blood, what did you see?"

For a long time Kye did not answer. It was as though he had turned his sight inwards and gone somewhere else. Though whether he was walking in the past, the future or the visions of the blood was anyone's guess.

When he eventually spoke, his voice seemed to come from a distance. "I saw a battlefield. I saw dead bodies, piled head high. I saw crows and wolves feasting on the dead. I saw clouds gathering and when it rained, it rained blood."

From out of the shadows, Eloo's whisper slivered. "The portents of war."

"But does that mean war will come?"

"Not necessarily," Lea sighed, "the spirits may simply be warning us of the threat of war."

"But war with whom? Who would war with us? The other lands are at peace with us."

"There is always the Darklings," Kye said, his eyes moving to where Eloo lay in his lap.

"The who?"

"They are what we call the dark side of our people," Eloo answered Rose, her voice sounding grim.

"But the Darklings were crushed in the last wars," Lightning said. "The orcs and their goblin kin were scattered to the four winds, after the battle of vale."

Rose was interested in what they said since she had been told about the orc wars by her father and her nurse. They told her the kingdom had been invaded by the dark elves and goblins, but that they had beaten them and the hordes of goblin monsters had been killed.

"But those wars were a hundred years ago," Rose pointed out.

"Exactly," Lea said.

"Exactly what?"

"What Lea means," Lightning said gently, "is a hundred years is enough time for such maggots to multiply."

"If they are the predicted enemy," Silver pointed out.

"Is there an easy way of finding out who it could be?"

"No army can assemble in complete secrecy," Lea said. Then a speculative look stole across his face. "There is always the Graeae."

"No, I will not deal with those hags," Eloo said, her voice almost steely.

"Why not? Your grandmother has them as her handmaidens," Lea said, pointedly.

"The crone queen must deal in darkness," Eloo spat back. "But I will not!"

84

"There are other forms of divination," Lor pointed out. "What about pyromancy? Lightning?"

"Sorry, Lor, I am not skilled enough for that," Lightning said, embarrassed, and seeing Rose's blank expression explained. "Pyromancy is a form of divination, but I am a third circle fire mage, and such secrets are only taught to higher ranks."

"But what about the Rod of Wisdom?" Lor asked. "Should we retrieve it, and if so how do we get into the tomb?"

"We must retrieve it," Silver said, before turning her back on the group and facing the tomb. "As for entering the tomb, that is something I can do."

"How?"

"By entering the spirit world," Silver said, her voice cold and emotionless.

Rose was seized by the image of another world. A wasteland, filled with hundreds of floating orbs and ghostly forms. She shuddered at the idea of willingly entering such a place.

"You should not go alone," Kye said, and made to rise.

"Stay," Silver said, her voice gentle, but still a command. "You are weak still, I shall go alone."

Without another word Silver Skin strode into the darkness and was gone, as though she had actually walked into another world. For a long time no one spoke, then Lightning broke the silence.

"Well, we had better settle in. Lor, any chance of some food?"

"Build up the fire and I shall see what I can do."

Lightning did so and soon there was a brace of rabbits cooking on the spit.

"How will Silver enter the spirit world?"

"She will leave her physical body and enter the spirit world that way," Lea said, and sensing Rose's next question he half raised a hand to stall her. "Please, Rose, don't ask me how she does so, it is a guarded secret."

"Then tell us something you can say," Lightning said. "Who built the citadel, do you know?"

THE ELF MOOT

"Elf Moots are rare events, it is not easy to gather the elves, and they do not take kindly to being ordered about."
Lea, from the Wereding Chronicles.

L ea considered Lightning's request, and after a moment staring into the fire he began to speak of the past.

"Since we are at the citadel, I will tell you of the Mutant wars, or at least what I know of them, for there are few who lived through those times and those who did wish to forget them. It is not known how the war started or exactly who took part in that war, but what we do know is the three heroes were involved. The witch sisters Heather and Holly combined their efforts with the Grey Pilgrim in the struggle against the Crimson Dragon and his children Sinner and The Dark Hunter..."

"Wait a moment, the Grey Pilgrim," Rose interrupted. "The same Grey Pilgrim of the scrolls?"

"Yes, Rose, the same," Lea said calmly, though he was clearly a little annoyed at being interrupted. "As I was saying, these three, possibly along with some of the fey, tried to stop the plan to unleash the mutant spawn on the world."

"I'm sorry to ask another question," Rose said, "but you are a Bard, Lea, don't you know which fey or who they were? Doesn't the Druid order know who they were?"

Lea did not answer for a long time, but glanced at Kye, as if asking him for permission to tell a secret. Kye shook his head and Lea turned his gaze back to the flames.

"I do not know, Rose," Lea said softly, as if he was still in the past, but Rose was convinced he was lying. He did know, but because of some family or druid secret he was not allowed to tell her. Still, when he began speaking again, she listened eagerly for she knew little of the wars before the great burning.

"I do not know, but I suspect some of the Silver Shield, perhaps even some of our family was there, but there is no record of it. Still, that is often the way, we prefer to work from the shadows."

"Lea," Kye growled, from where he was charging his pipe, as though he was warning Lea he was giving too much away.

"The Crimson Dragon used magic and science which is lost to us now, to create this army of mutants that spread the mutating disease like a plague. The three heroes tried to destroy this plague, but they must have only been partially successful. For as we know they spread their disease across the world as it was then and it led to the great burning."

"Do we know that?"

"Not for sure," Lea conceded, flicking a twig into the flames. "But we do know one thing followed another, we know that. Still, even if the great burning did not follow directly, what we do know is that although the three evil ones were defeated, the three heroes died in the attempt and were entombed here."

"But if they all died, who built the tomb, and when?"

Once again Lea glanced in Kye's direction, but he was sitting back from the fire and since his pipe had gone out Rose could not see his face.

"Once again, Rose, you ask a question I do not know the answer to."

"What do you know?"

"The Threefold Crimson One rose to burn the world with his poison," Lea began to chant. "He summoned a monstrous daughter and bade her breed a race of monsters. She lay with her brother, the Dark Hunter, who with his deadly dart and dark heart led an army of demons to ravage the earth. Against them stood the Three – Grey, Heather and Holly – they who wove a spell to banish the storm and summon the form of nature. They drove back the storm, but perished in the deed. Where their spirits dwell now we cannot say, but their bodies were laid in walls of stone and a spell wove strong in the long barrow of the citadel. That is what the Bards know of the history of the mutant wars."

"That's..." Rose might have said beautiful, but that was not the right word. "Sad."

"Perhaps," Lea said, charging his pipe. "The Bards are charged with remembering and recording in song and poetry what passes in the world."

"They didn't do a very good job this time, did they?" Lightning said, tossing a bone into the fire.

"They do what they can," said Lea haughtily. "We are supposed to remember what passes in the world, but we cannot record what we do not know."

"Excuses..."

"Enough," Eloo snapped, her green eyes gleaming like those of a cat in the dark. "Silver is returning. Lor, she will need food and a warm drink."

Lor leapt from where he was sitting by Lea and began to refill the kettle. The others stood and stared towards the citadel, but saw nothing.

"Are you sure, Eloo?"

Eloo did not answer, she seemed to have gone somewhere else, but Silver appeared out of the dark, as though the night had given birth to her. Her eyes glowed yellow and her tall form bent as if under a weight. Her steps were slow and uncertain, her hair appearing grey and not black in the flickering light and she leant heavily on her wooden staff. Kye gazed into her face and nodded. He gave Silver a flask and with Lea's help, they led her to the fire where she sat staring into the hot embers. Her face appeared transparent, as if it were only half formed and her body was as much a lamp through which her spirit burnt.

"Is she going to be all right?"

"She'll be fine in time," Lor said, as he forced a mug into her hands. "The spirit world has an aging effect, even to us, but she will be as normal in the morning."

"And in the morning we must return to Care Diff," said Eloo in a faraway voice.

"But why?" Lea asked.

"My mother has called me," Eloo said, in an equally distant voice. "There is to be an Elf Moot, we are summoned to the court."

"A Moot," Lea said, his voice sounded surprised. "But there hasn't been a Moot in a hundred years, why now?"

"Perhaps they know what we do?"

"Does the horned queen say why?"

"No, only that I should go, and bring Rose with me."

"They want me at the Elven court?"

"It would appear even Selene has heard of you," Kye said, his yellow eyes fixing Rose with a stare that felt as if it would pierce her to the bone and it certainly chilled her to the bone.

"What of the wand?"

Silver lifted from beside her a long rod that glinted in the firelight.

Rose moved closer, to get a better look at it. The wand was a long staff about four feet long, and was tipped with metal points. Mounted on the wand were multiple rings of metal, inscribed with runes and strange symbols. Rose stared at the runes and felt a strange lethargy fall over her mind, as though someone had drawn a veil across it. In this daze she watched her hand reach out and touch the wand.

As her hand touched the tip of the staff, the metal rings circling the wand's core began to move, twisting and circling into new positions. Rose could see new parts of the inscribed metal. Now the rings displayed different runes and suddenly Rose heard herself speaking in a strange tongue. As she spoke, the fire beside them flared up. Then the fire blinked out and Rose was on her knees, both hands locked round the wand, Silver staring at her through a veil of tears.

"Robin!" Rose heard herself whisper.

"What just happened?" Lightning asked, as his strong arm wrapped around Rose's shoulders and pulled her away from the wand.

"Rose just used the wand to perform a scrying spell," Eloo said, her voice full of the surprise and shock Rose felt.

"But Rose has already told me she knows no magic," Lightning said, holding Rose close, his body providing her with surprising strength. "Silver, do you know how this is possible?"

"As for the earlier incident I am not sure yet," Silver said, her voice carrying the weight of her fatigue. "However, the wand is supposed to be used in just the way Rose used it. A person may tap into the magic of the wand and make it reveal the spell they require. Rose wanted to see her sister, so the wand showed her a scrying spell.

"Though as to the wisdom of such a casting I am not so sure. It might have been better if she had not used the wand and yet, and yet..."

"Was that Robin I saw?" Rose croaked, gathering strength from Lightning's warming presence. "But what was she doing in black robes?"

"Black robes?" Kye asked suddenly, his voice harsh, his face a stone mask. "Was she wearing any kind of necklace, or brooch?"

Rose was taken aback by this question and had to concentrate hard to call the vision to her mind's eye.

"A ring made of red metal, on a similar chain," Rose said, her brow wrinkling with puzzlement. Her sister had never been one for necklaces or anything like that; she was more of a tomboy.

She was brought out of her puzzlement by Silver's sharp question. "Was she holding anything?"

"A staff of black metal, I think."

Rose glanced up from the embers of the fire, to catch a glance pass from Kye to Silver, and her instincts told her they knew something about what she had seen and they didn't like it.

"Why, what is wrong? Is Robin in danger or something?"

Rose watched, as once again a silent thought passed between the two werewolves. This sight of what appeared to be either a lie or at least a refusal to answer lit the fires of frustration in Rose.

She gave vent to her frustration. "What the hell do I have to do to get a straight answer around here? Will someone please tell me, what is wrong? What trouble is Robin in?"

Rose's rage was stalled by the sound of Eloo's laughter that rumbled out of her tiny form, deep and powerful like distant thunder.

"What's so funny?" Rose asked, between gritted teeth.

"Not you," Eloo tried to say, though she was still hiccupping with laughter. "It's just the idea of a werewolf and particularly a Druid giving you a straight answer is hilarious..."

Even Lightning sniggered at this, that was until Rose looked over her shoulder and gave him a sobering glare.

"Rose," Silver said, her face grim. "Contrary to what Eloo says, I will give you a straight answer – if there is such a thing."

"That is a debate for another day," Lightning cut in, as if he would stall any such debate.

"If Kye or I do not tell you everything we know, it is to protect you."

"In case you didn't notice, I am a big girl."

"That is a matter of opinion," Kye muttered, but did not flinch when Rose glared at him.

"The truth, Rose, is that we do not know for certain what trouble your sister has gotten herself into," Silver said, her gaze level and unflinching. "But we suspect she has been recruited into the ranks of the Crimson Circle."

"The who?"

Rose's question was apparently unexpected, as Silver's eyebrows almost disappeared into her silvery hairline.

"You have never heard of them? My, haven't lived had a sheltered life!"

"A blessed one," muttered Kye.

"So who are they and how are they bad news for Robin?"

"The Crimson Circle are a brotherhood, a society of dark magic users, who have made pacts with the dark powers to grant them earthly and political power, in your society. If your sister has been made a member it means she is mixed up with some very dark characters."

"But magic is banned in the city states."

"And who do you think got that ban imposed?" Lea asked, as he drank from a wine skin.

"But if they use magic, why would they make such a ban?"

"So everyone but they are forbidden from using magic," Lightning said between gulps of the wine.

Rose declined the skin and paced up and down before the dying fire. When she came to a stop, it was to find both Kye and Silver Skin watching her, their eyes once more plumbing the depths of her soul.

"Let me get this right. Robin could be mixed up with dark magic users, that means what?"

"That she herself could be a dark magic user," Kye said, his voice hard as a winter's black frost.

Rose felt a hand of ice grip her heart. The one thing her father had always feared and warned them against was meddling in magic, especially dark magic. The thought of Robin dabbling in dark magic made Rose feel sick. On the other hand, she herself had performed magic, what would her father think of that? She shook her head.

She could not explain that, could she be blamed for it if she did not know how she was doing it? Then Rose saw before her mind's eye Robin in the dark robes and now she realised a detail she had not noticed before. There was an expression on her sister's face, one Rose had not seen before. It was one that twisted her familiar face. It was a look of hate.

"If, if you're right," Rose said hesitantly, unwilling to accept their analysis, "can we save her?"

"There may be a way," Silver said, her voice unsure. "But if we are to save her, we must get her away from the people who now influence her and we cannot do that yet. We must attend the Moot first."

"But why? We have to save Robin!"

"Rose," Kye said, standing so his face could be clearly seen, his eyes staring into Rose's, his expression for once clear and readable. It was a look of sincerity. "Rose, I know you do not know me, but I ask you to trust me now. We will do everything in our power to help your sister. The Crimson circle are our enemies, too. But your sister will be in one of the cities and we cannot get to her now. We will put out the word to our embassies in the city and as soon as we know where your sister is, we will help you to help her."

Rose stared into his eyes and although she wanted to disbelieve him, she could not bring herself to. She did not know him, but something in her heart was telling her he was not lying. Still, her soul still cried out for Robin. She wanted her sister here now and safe from any dark magic user. This made her re-evaluate her thoughts. She was wanting her sister to be in the company of werewolves and elves. Days ago, that would have been to her mind the worst fate imaginable. Still, although these people seemed wild and unpredictable at times, her heart if not her mind told her they were not evil.

She turned from Kye to find Lightning watching her. She met his eyes and knew he was not evil. No, not evil, and yet there was something about him that told her she had only seen part of his face. Still, she felt she could trust him, she already knew that.

From behind her, Kye spoke. "Rose, I swear to you, in the name of the Silver Lady, that if your sister can be saved, she will be."

"But why would you swear?" Rose asked, not looking at him, her eyes fixed on Lightning.

"For several reasons," Silver answered, for her brother and probably the whole company. "For one, it is the right thing to do. For another, the crimson circle are our sworn enemies and one less member is a good thing. But for the most important reason of all, she is your sister and she is the other part of your heart."

Silver's words mirrored Rose's thoughts and feelings. Robin is not here, her heart cried out and tears sprang to her eyes. "I need her,"

Rose whispered, her voice breaking with the pain welling up from her heart. The pain she felt breaking over her like a wave. She broke down, sobbing into Lightning's chest as his strong arms wrapped around her.

When Rose came back to herself, it was to find Lightning embracing her and a strong hand gripping both shoulders. Rose, feeling embraced, peered over her shoulders to find both Kye and Silver standing behind her, a hand on each shoulder, their eyes watching her grief with compassion.

"I am sorry, I didn't mean to do that," Rose sniffled, her face flushed with embarrassment.

The two werewolves did not speak, but nodded sagely.

"What now?"

"We will have another tea and then turn in and rise early for another march to Care Diff," Silver said, and replaced the kettle on the fire.

They did as she advised, Rose wrapping herself in the cloak Lightning gave her and lying as close to the fire as she could get, lying her head on the pillow of her arm. Eloo curled up by Kye's side, her head in his lap as he wrapped himself in his cloak and continued to smoke his pipe, as if he would sit up for a long time. Perhaps he had set himself the duty of guard.

Silver must have changed when Rose wasn't watching, for her huge wolf form glittered in the moonlight, her legs and head glowing silver, a stark contrast to her dark body. If Rose were more awake she might have stared longer at the beautiful, if scary wolf, but she could hardly keep her eyes open and even as she yawned, the huge wolf loped into the trees. Rose did not see where the twins were, as sleep came down and wrapped her in its oblivious arms.

Rose was woken by Lightning, in the dim light of dawn. His cup of tea did not quite drive out the chill of the predawn mist that hung thick about the clearing.

"How far is this place we are making for?"

"Three day's march," replied Silver, who despite being absent the night before looked refreshed and untouched by the events of the previous day.

"Then we had better get a move on, hadn't we?" Lea said, removing the kettle from the fire.

"Breakfast first," Eloo said, ladling a thick porridge from the kettle.

After Rose ate the porridge, which was surprisingly good and sweetened with honey, Kye stamped out the fire and they set out, retracing their steps of the previous day, though not at such a quick pace. Rose guessed this was to conserve their strength as they had a greater distance to go.

"Are we returning to the meeting place and the armoury?" Rose asked Lightning.

"We are heading in that direction," Lightning said as he strode along at her side, "but we will cross back onto the other bank and head close to Kye's tree house and cut north to the care."

No one spoke for a long time, as they strode along the river bank, until Rose realised the twins were no longer with them.

"Where are the twins?"

"Now she notices," snorted Kye.

"They left after breakfast and headed off to find and inform the rest of the pack the news of the Moot," Silver explained.

"Though they already know, unless I miss my guess," Eloo said softly.

"Great Mother should have heard the call," Kye said.

This talk of a call piqued Rose's curiosity, an easy thing to do.

"Eloo what call is this, I heard nothing?"

"No, you wouldn't have," Eloo said, jogging along behind Kye. "My mother talked to my mind and you are not skilled in telepathy, or you would have heard her call. Kye, how about a bite at the next bend?"

Kye did not respond, but as Eloo had asked at the next wide curve of the river he halted and handed out a large amount of whey-bread which he produced from his pack. Rose took the heavy biscuit like substance with reluctance. She had eaten the stuff before on hunts with her father and it had always been a filling, if tasteless food that filled the belly but did not please the tongue. This, like much of the food Kye provided, was surprisingly good, for it was not the hardtack she was expecting it to be. Unlike the usual hardtack, this whey-bread had dried fruits mixed in with the oats that made up the bread.

"This is the best I've had," she said, eagerly demolishing the food.

Kye gave a half smile, and as if rewarding her for the flattery handed her a second portion. As they were refilling their water bottles the twins re-joined them, appearing out of the trees before them. With them was an unexpected, but welcome friend.

"Cloud!" Lightning and Rose cried almost at once and the horse whinnied as the two rushed forward to meet him.

"We found him a few miles north," Lea said, accepting a chunk of whey-bread from Kye.

"Were you looking for me?" Lightning said to the horse, feeding it a chunk of his own whey-bread.

Rose would not at this moment have been surprised if the horse had answered in a voice, but if he could speak he at this moment preferred to munch on the biscuit.

"Cloud seems to like your whey-bread as much as I do," Rose said cheekily to Kye, who grunted and turned his attention to his younger brother.

"Lor, did you speak to the pack?"

"Yus," Lor confirmed his question through a mouthful of the bread. "She is waiting for the rest of the pack before setting out. They should be half a day behind us at the most."

"Then let's get on." Kye turned and continued to lead them, back towards the place they had started from.

"Is it much further?" Rose asked, noticing the shadows growing.

"A few thousand yards I think," Lightning said as he led Cloud by his bridle. "Are you tired? Would you like to mount?"

"No, it's fine. I was just thinking of the time."

"Let Kye think about the time."

Rose was letting Kye bother about the time. What she was worrying about was the fact that every step brought her closer to the Elven court, and what she would see at the court both excited her and stirred deep fears.

"Lightning, what is this Moot we are going to?"

"What do you think it is?"

"The Elven court?"

"Correct, the queen of the elves, Selene, has called a Moot. She and her kin and their king the Horned god often hold court and make rulings on our people, but a Moot is different."

"How different?"

"A Moot is what you might call a special meeting and requires every fey to attend. As Lor says, there hasn't been a Moot for hundreds of years. They are usually only called if there is some great threat to the people of the nations."

"Who will be there?"

"Werewolves, like the pack, elves of course..."

"Like Eloo?"

"Yes, though Eloo is only one kind of elf, so that is no example."

"I'm sorry, I don't understand."

"I'll explain later, but for now, who else will be there. Furies, of course..."

"Furies?"

"The Queen's bodyguard. As the Silver Shield is the King's bodyguard the Furies are the Queen's. They, like the Silver Shield, have centaurs amongst them though they are of course female, and among them are Furies themselves."

"What are Furies, when they are at home?"

"Well bless my beard! They don't teach you much about our ways! Furies are cat like centaurs. They have the lower body of great cats and human, well, a woman's body above. Like and yet unlike centaurs."

This description conjured for Rose an image of a huge lion's body with an amazon's body sprouting from the creature's neck.

"Are there many of these creatures?"

"Many? I suppose that depends on what you mean by many. There are perhaps a hundred of them in all; no one has ever counted them. After all, no one has ever counted any of the nations."

"So what else will be there?"

"You mean who else," Lightning gently corrected her.

"Yes, I mean who," Rose said, blushing at the mistake.

"There will be the Heorotaura, stag centaurs and perhaps my people will be there."

This statement confused Rose. 'My people', what did Lightning mean, his people? He was human, wasn't he? She glanced at him, searching for pointed ears or anything that she might find on Eloo's body, but in this light he appeared normal, if normal was the word. Was it? After all, Eloo was an elf, and even with or perhaps because of the strange looking ears and everything else, she still appeared beautiful to Rose. Rose wondered if she should ask him outright what he meant, but did she really want to find out? She was wondering this as Kye stopped suddenly.

They had re-crossed the Trespasser and were approaching a small hill, when Kye halted in his tracks, his eyes fixed at a point on the ground just at his feet.

"What is it, Kye?" Lor asked, crowding Kye's shoulder.

Kye did not answer, but warned Lor off and went down on his haunches to better see the ground before him, sniffing the earth.

"What is he looking for?"

"I do not know," Lightning said, craning his neck to see around the other in front of him. "Kye is a Stone Talker."

Rose realised that this information did not surprise her. Everything Kye did made him seem the very example of the Druid's soldier.

As Rose watched Kye with his eyes inches from the ground, she remembered what she had been told about the Stone Talkers. There was not a lot she could remember, but there was not a lot known about the shadowy Druid order. Their name came from the legend that they could track anything and could follow trails invisible to others. This was possible because they could talk to the very stones.

Watching Kye, Rose could believe it.

Kye rose with that wild grace that accompanied every action and though he did not move a step, he seemed to be casting about for something, as though he expected to find some sign hidden to the rest of them. After a few moments, he moved away and up the hill and then he returned, an expression of grim alertness on his face.

"Lor, tell me what you see."

Lor bent over the spot Kye was pointing at. Rose could now see the ground. It was a small dell at the foot of the hill where a trickle of water bled from the side of the hill to soften the earth and turn it slightly boggy. In the softened earth was impressed the clear print of a large boot.

"I'm guessing it's not Kye's?"

"Haven't you noticed the werewolves' footprints?"

"I can't say I've seen one."

"That, my beautiful Rose, is the point; they don't leave any."

"Any more?" Lor asked, his eyes flicking about him.

"The grass is trampled on the passing place, but no more tracks."

"Conclusion?"

"Someone has come through and moved off towards the north," Kye said, his eyes staring over their heads and into the distance, as if searching for this strange leaver of tracks.

"No scent?" Eloo asked, as if Kye could smell like a tracking dog.

Though when Rose came to think about that, Kye being a werewolf might have senses denied to her. On the heels of that thought came the question, what did she smell like to him?

"Only our own."

"It could be one of the nation coming for the Moot," Eloo pointed out.

Kye did not answer, but his tense, spear-straight stance implied he did not buy that. Still, after a long glance north he turned aside and continued to lead them to the tree house, where they all tiredly climbed the rope ladder to find Eloo stoking a small fire on the hearth stone.

"We will go on tomorrow," Silver said, and laid a pot on the hearth. "We have come a little out of our way, but as night has fallen it makes sense for us to rest here until tomorrow, if Eloo and Kye have no objections to us sharing their tree house?"

"My dear Silver, what is mine is yours," Eloo said, bowing low, a grin on her lips.

Kye, for his part, did not as usual answer with words, but instead held out a bottle for Silver to drink from. Rose was relieved to be off her feet, for the march was taking its toll and she was glad to pull her boots off and let them dangle over the edge of the planks that formed the house floor. Rose was surprised when Lor dropped down beside her, his feet bare.

"It feels good to let the air get to them every now and again," he said and handed her a bowl of steaming stew.

"Thanks. When do we start tomorrow?"

"Probably before dawn," Lor yawned. "Kye will want to start as soon as he can, so it's an early night for you, young lady."

Rose was about to protest at the 'young lady' when she realised that if Lor was even half Kye's age, it made her a very young lady from his point of view.

Once they finished the stew, they gathered round the fire and listened to Eloo sing in a language Rose had never heard before, which was soft and sweet and acted like a lullaby that swept her into a dreamless sleep.

The next thing Rose knew was Kye standing over her, a bowl of porridge in one hand, a mug of tea in the other.

"Is it time already?" She yawned and accepted his gifts.

After breakfast the party set off heading north, through ever deeper and deeper woods. When the dawn came, it found Rose amongst tall oaks and ash trees that gleamed wetly in a cold dawn.

"Do the woods stretch all the way to the North?"

"They did once," Silver said, a dreamy look in her eyes, "but that was many thousands of years ago, before the last civilisation. No, these woods go on for a few more miles and then we come to the grey desert."

"And what's that?"

"Have you never seen a map of this area?"

"No, my father had one I think, but he would not let us see it."

"Well, maps aside, the Grey Desert is a patch of ruins from the great burning. They lie between us and the Care."

"They don't sound very inviting."

"They are a horrible wasteland, where nothing grows," Silver said, visibly shuddering. "If we could avoid them we would, but they are the quickest way to the Moot."

"Lightning, have you been there before?"

"No, I have always avoided it, but I believe Kye has passed through that region several times."

"Why would he?"

"Kye is a Stone Talker, a soldier of the druid order. He must protect us from evil things and his duties have taken him to many strange places."

"Why haven't I heard about this?"

"Well, for a start, I was under the impression that the Druids were a loathed organisation in your lands. So the exploits of the Druids, let alone the Talkers, would not be welcome. Secondly, the Talkers work in secret. They do not like anyone to know what they do."

"Why?"

"Because it is our nature," Lor, who was bringing up the rear of the column said. "We are Stone Talkers and water people. It is our nature to know what others do not and to make sure they do not fall into the wrong hands. We keep our secrets."

"But if my people knew this they might not..." Rose broke off, suddenly aware that she was broaching a subject she herself shared in.

"Hate us," Lightning said, laughing at Rose's expression. "Sorry Rose, I am ribbing you!"

"Hush," came Kye's harsh whisper.

Rose decided to keep silent and look about her. The trees seemed to march on forever, their trunks like pillars of great halls. Their branches stretched above them like a huge roof, but this hall was not a quiet one. For there were countless birds in the upper branches and sweet voices twittered and whistled in Rose's ear. Once there was a flash of red against the brown of a tree's trunk and Rose realised that a red squirrel had just leapt across their path.

At a rest stop in a small clearing, Rose saw something that surprised her. A large fox, bright in his red coat, trotted out of the trees and not fleeing at the sight of them, trotted up to Kye, who for his part, knelt to listen carefully to its barks. He answered it with a bark and after giving it a rabbit to carry off in its jaws, the animal trotted tail held high back into the wall of the trees.

"Is there any animal Kye can't speak to?"

"There must be some," Eloo said, and passed Kye a water skin. "But it was a fox and theirs and the wolf tongue are similar."

"What did he tell you, Kye?"

"That the woods ahead are clear and that as far as he knows the rivers have not flooded."

"Have any of the pack passed this way?"

"He has not seen them, if they have."

"How far away is the desert?"

"We will reach it by dusk."

"Will we cross today?"

"Not if we can help it. I would prefer to cross it in daylight, if possible."

"Can we not reach it sooner?"

"Only if we double our pace."

"We could change and the others could ride."

"We could, Lea, but that would mean leaving some of our weapons here and I fear we may need them in the Grey Desert."

"Why, what may we need them for?"

"I hope there will be no need, Rose, but I would be a fool if I did not fear goblins or worse in that accursed place."

"Then we shall proceed as we can. Kye, lead on."

THE GREY DESERT

"The night holds many horrors, but none worse than what the mind can imagine."
The Book of the Wolf.

The trees slowly began to thin, their canopy breaking as the height and number diminished. The sun was soon casting dappled light on their faces. Then the trees disappeared, giving way to fallen and rotting trunks and stumps. They, in turn, gave way to tall grasses that disappeared a dozen feet off the tree line.

The grass did not simply dwindle, but disappeared and not a blade grew beyond this point. The Grey Desert was a good name for the wasteland that lay before them. The grass gave way to grey, stony ground, dusty though not sandy, and devoid of grass or seed and it stretched flat for hundreds of yards, until rising in the distance was a low range of saw toothed hills.

"How are we for water?"

"We will have enough to last us for the next few days," Lea said, recapping his water bottle.

"Good, because even if we find any water in there, we cannot drink it," Kye said, drawing something from his pack.

"What is that?"

Rose saw with amazement that Kye had an instrument her father had considered the height of his collection. "A telescope!"

"Yes," Kye said, surprised at her exclamation. "Most of the shield have the spyglass. Why do you seem so surprised?"

"Because my father spent a large amount of money to obtain one. I thought there weren't more than a handful left, from the time of the burning."

"In the lands of humans," Silver said, "but we saved many instruments from that time."

"What do you see, Kye?"

"Nothing appears to be moving," Kye answered, and passed the brass tube to Lor.

"Did you expect there to be?"

"No, but it doesn't hurt to check."

"Rose, perhaps you would like a try?" Lor said, offering her the telescope.

Rose gingerly took the glass and placed it to her eye. Squinting, she stared through the eye piece, to see the hills on the horizon. They leapt out at her and she could see now that they were not hills, but the ruins of once great buildings, several storeys high. They must have been taller than that at one time, but some disaster wrecked them, for they were jagged and broken, as if gales of wind had ripped the top off them.

"What were they?" Rose asked, and handed the glass back to Kye.

"They were once the towers of the last world, but now they are nothing but the bones of a dead beast."

"Do we proceed?"

Kye turned to Silver and their shared look told Rose that they were consulting with one another. Though whether they were communicating telepathically or not she could not say. After a few moments, Kye turned away and Silver turned to the rest of the group.

"We will not cross tonight," she told them as Kye moved onto the grey ground. "We will start again tomorrow."

"Where is Kye going?" Rose asked, watching him lie on the ground, his ear pressed to the hard dirt.

"He is seeing if he can hear anything and is probably only getting an earful of your beautiful voice," Lightning said, grinning from ear to ear. "Come let's give him a chance and find a camp site."

Lor led the party several hundred yards back into the woods, finding a small but pleasant clearing with a little brook bubbling through it and it was here that they made camp.

Lightning had just lit a small fire and was boiling up tea when Kye appeared at Rose's shoulder. He appeared like a ghost, silent and unexpected, and Rose gasped with surprise as he seemingly materialised out of thin air.

"Anything?" Silver asked in an unruffled voice, as if Kye's materialisation had not surprised her.

"Something might be stirring in the bowels of the earth," Kye answered, accepting a mug from Eloo. "But what it is and where it is I cannot say."

"Who is to take the first watch?"

"I will, and Lor after me," Kye grunted, between gulps.

"What about the fire?"

"So long as it doesn't smoke," Kye said, staring towards the desert. "But once the night falls it might be best that we don't show a light."

"Will it be good not to have light so close to the desert?"

"The moon is only just beginning to wane. There should be enough light to see, even for Rose."

"Then we had better have a hot meal, while we can."

They ate the usual stew washed down with stream water and finished off with more of Kye's bread. While the rest of the party wrapped themselves in cloaks and blankets, Kye filled his pipe and stood guard on the northern side of the clearing.

"Lightning," Rose asked hesitantly, not sure she really wanted to know the answer. "What are you?"

"I beg your pardon?"

"Well, Eloo is an elf, the others are werewolves, so what are you?"

"What a personal question," Lightning said in a grave voice and then he laughed. "There's hope for you yet."

"You don't mind me asking?"

"Not in the least. However, the answer is something I cannot, for the moment, divulge."

Rose did not quite know how to respond to this, so she let the silence stretch in the hope that it might force Lightning into speaking.

"I would like to answer your question, Rose," Lightning said, his manner suddenly hesitant. "I would like to tell you, but I am afraid that I am not allowed to."

"More secrets," Rose snarled. "Then tell me something you can say."

"Would you like to know how to start fires by clicking your fingers?"

Rose was intrigued, feeling mixed emotions surge through her. She was both eager and fearful to learn magic.

"So do you want to learn a spell or not?"

"Can I do magic?"

"Let's see."

Lightning placed a small pile of twigs in front of Rose and

gestured to it.

"See if you can ignite that."

"How?"

"With the magic words, incendium."

"Incendum."

"No, incendium," Lightning corrected.

"Incendium. Is that all?"

"No, with the words you must make these gestures," Lightning said, and made a twisting gesture with his left hand while drawing a circle with the other.

"Like this?" Rose asked, trying to mirror him and finding it difficult to concentrate on both hands at once, as they tried to perform the strange movements.

"A little more expansive."

"Incendium," Rose whispered, and made the gestures, but nothing happened. "I can't do it!"

"Well, you didn't expect to do it just like that, did you?"

"Actually, yes."

Lightning laughed, and Rose couldn't help herself, she too laughed.

"Okay, there is one part of spell casting I forgot to mention."

"You're holding out on me!"

"No, I promise, it's just that I forgot you've never done anything like this before."

"So what am I missing?"

"Magic is an energy. It has to have a power source. You have to summon your inner energies."

"And how do I do this?"

"Close your eyes and concentrate hard. Imagine a well of water and then imagine you are drawing water up from that well, and then cast the spell."

Rose did what Lightning suggested. Closing her eyes, she imagined a deep well of cool water and she visualised water rising through the air. As she did this, she slowly spoke the words and performed the gestures. Against her closed eyes, there flared a bright light.

"You did it!"

Rose opened her eyes, to see that the small pile of twigs had burst into flames and a thin curl of smoke was rising through the air. Eloo, who had unnoticed by Rose moved up behind her, doused the small fire with her mug of tea.

"Well done," Lightning said, his voice bursting with delight.

Rose smiled tiredly, for now she felt an overwhelming fatigue and could hardly keep her eyes open.

"I cast a spell," she yawned.

"Yes, you did," Eloo said, and placed a rolled up cloak as a pillow under Rose's heavy head. "Now sleep, and you will be all refreshed in the morning."

As if this was a command, Rose was fast asleep and snoring gently.

Eloo, who was standing by Rose's head, glanced from her innocent face to the scorched twigs to Lightning and back again to Rose.

"Is it wise to teach her magic?"

"Why wouldn't it be?"

"Because we do not know what her part is yet."

"Do you know?"

Eloo cocked her head at that and grinned. "Perhaps."

"She is not evil," Lightning said, his chin rising, eyes glowing brilliantly.

"Did I say so?" Eloo's look of speculation broke into a sunburst smile. "I myself have healed her. I know her, she is not evil."

Lightning smiled back at her. "Then why warn me about teaching her magic?"

"Because her destiny is uncertain."

"Eloo may be right to caution you, Lightning," Silver said, standing over Rose. "She used the wand unknowingly and in doing so stirred magics that have not been disturbed in a long time."

"What do you guess?"

"I am not sure of this myself," Silver said, slowly. "But I believe there is magic in Rose and when the Fire Drake attacked her, it awoke."

"What magic?"

Silver raised a hand to warn off Lightning and she bowed her head.

"I am sorry, but I cannot answer your questions, Lightning, because I do not know the answers. I only know that I have suspicions and one of them is that Rose may be more than she appears. We should tread carefully when it comes to giving her magic."

"Well, let's sleep on it," Eloo said, yawning largely. "Some questions answer themselves with the morning light."

AMONG THE RUINS

"Ruins are not always dead."
The Wereding Chronicles, by the Red Wizard.

Rose woke to find a dull, dim day that was more night than day.

"Is it dawn?"

"It should be, but as you can see this front is hiding the sun," Lor said as he boiled porridge in his kettle.

Rose glanced again at the sky that was visible through the tree branches. A cloud bank had rolled up and was hanging low over everything.

"Is it going to rain?"

"It doesn't feel like rain," Silver said, and scribbled something in a scroll.

"What are you doing?"

"Making a report of our progress, so the clan know where we are."

"But how will they get it?"

"He will take it to them," Silver said, indicating a large raven pecking at the ground nearby.

Rose watched as the bird fluttered over to Silver and stood on one leg, as Silver tied the scroll to its leg. Cocking its head to look at her, it cried and went flapping into the sky. As the bird flew away, Kye appeared on the other side of the clearing. His hair and cape glistened with dew drops, his face a closed mask. Rose would not have been able to read that inscrutable face a few days before, but now she thought she could read some of his manner and his ramrod stance told her that he was not happy about something.

"Find anything?"

Kye shook his head, and sinking down beside Eloo, gently shook her awake and said something to her Rose could not hear. She watched with fascination as Eloo stretched, yawning like a large cat.

As she awoke, she rubbed herself up against Kye, who picked her up in his arms and carried her to the spring, where she could wash herself.

"Silver, what lies on the other side of the ruins?"

"A great hedge, that acts as a barrier between the woods and the Grey Desert."

"And how do we get through this hedge?"

"There is a gate that usually has a guard."

"Usually?"

"Even they may have been drawn away by the call to the Moot."

"If they have, could that be a problem?"

"We will see."

"Well if we are to see, we had better make a start."

After a quick breakfast they moved out, returning to the spot they had been at the night before – the grey, cracked land that stretched away to the hill buildings, though now Rose could not see them, for all she could see was the ceiling of clouds that pressed down on them as though it would press them into the lifeless earth.

"What will we find in there?"

"Who can say?"

"Kye?"

Kye, who had been staring into the distance, turned to face them, his eyes sweeping each face. "If we are lucky, only the ruins."

"And if we aren't?"

"There have not been goblins or orcs here for many years, but their numbers have been growing."

"What about drakes?"

"I pray to the Lady not," Silver said.

"Try to stay in the open at all times and keep going north and we may be all right." Without another word, Kye strung his bow, fit an arrow to the string and led them out onto the grey, dry and cracked earth that was the Grey Desert.

For about an hour the land was unchanging, dead and featureless. Then it began to show the first signs of civilisation, or a civilisation that had been. The first thing Rose noticed about the change was the sound of her footfalls. Her footsteps had sounded flat and toneless, as if the earth was swallowing them up. Then they changed to a deeper thud and checking, Rose saw that the ground had changed from dry dirt to stone. On closer inspection she realised that they were standing on a cracked substance like stone, but which she did not recognise.

"This was a road!"

"Once."

"But it isn't made of stone!"

"No," Silver said, and tapped it with her staff. "The last world had other materials than stone to build with."

"But what is it?"

"Does it matter at this moment?"

"I suppose not," Rose admitted, though she would still like to know. "Does it lead us through the ruins?"

"It leads us in," Silver admitted reluctantly. "But whether it leads us out, only time will tell."

"Shush," Kye hissed, and stooped low to the ground, his ear all but pressed to the earth.

"What is it, Kye?" Eloo asked, bending over him.

"There is a vibration," Kye said softly. "Can't you hear it?"

Rose strained her ears, but for a long time she couldn't hear anything. Then she felt, more than heard it. It was like a tremor that came and went every few minutes and then it was gone, as if it never existed.

"What is it?"

"I do not know," Kye said, straightening, his eyes scanning all around him. "I have been through these lands many times, but have never heard this."

"What could it mean?"

Kye did not or could not answer. He simply shook his head and led on, though at a slower pace. Soon after this, they came across more signs of the culture that had been. Broken stones and rusting metalwork thrust up like the bones of some ancient animal. Rose stared at them and shuddered as she wondered what they had been. Then they came across a rusting metal hulk.

"What was that?"

"It appears to be a metal carriage," Lightning said, pointing at the remains of a wheel with his walking stick.

"They called it a car," Lea said, from behind them.

"But what drew it, there are no shafts?"

"They could have rusted away," Lightning suggested, as they moved forwards.

"It was not drawn by horses," Lea said, throwing a glance over his shoulder at the rusting wreck. "It had its own engine, that burnt fuel."

"I've heard of those," Rose said, wrinkling her forehead as she tried to recall the name her father had used when pointing one out to her. "A locomotive."

"No, it was not steam power," Lea said. "It was a petroleum burning engine."

"A what?"

"A derivative of fossil fuels."

"I have not heard of that."

"What history do you know, Rose?"

"You two," Silver said, turning on them, her expression stern. "Now is neither the time, nor the place for history lessons. Come, let us move on, we can talk history later."

Rose was not sure about that, for as they moved among more ruins she wondered where would be a better place to discuss history.

They passed more wrecks of the "cars", and eventually they reached the remains of a structure. It was a small building, but must have been more than one storey, as its walls were jagged like the battlements of some castle that had sunk below the earth. Another building beyond this had been demolished entirely, for the ground opened up and the party found themselves gazing down into a basement area below ground level that was full of rubble, and Rose shivered seeing among them several skulls. Skulls that were blackened as though fierce heat had scorched them.

"What did this to them?"

"The time of Burning," Silver said, and touched her charms and necklaces.

"The heat, though," Lightning said, his voice awed. "Some of those bricks appear to have been turned to glass."

"If the druids know," Lea said glancing at Silver, "they are not saying."

"Let's hustle, people," Lor said, casting about, like Kye, his bow strung and loaded.

The party moved deeper into the ruins, coming across more walls and rusted cars, but although the walls rose steadily they did not seem to rise above the first storey, until the road they were following led them into a large square, or meeting of roads. Behind them sprawled the broken walls, but in front of them on three sides there spread massive walls that towered up above them, though their tops too, were broken and the windows that pierced the walls gaped darkly, like sightless eyes. This place should have been lit by the sun, but a dark cloud cover hung just above the tops of the towers and the square appeared dark and grey in the long shadows cast by the buildings.

"I don't like the look of this place," Lor muttered, his voice pitched low, but in the motionless air of the ruins it echoed off the walls.

"Be still," Kye hissed.

"Kye, do you know this place?"

Kye did not answer Rose's question. Instead he motioned for them to stay where they were, in the shadow of the buildings that served as entrance to the square. He slowly crept forward, until he was near the middle of the square where he took shelter behind the silent and empty pedestal of what might have once been a fountain.

From behind this stone wall he scanned the dark walls and the exits that were open to him.

From where Rose stood with Lightning it appeared they could either continue straight forward and pass through an archway that joined the buildings, while allowing the road to pass under them, or they could follow one of the other roads that led left or right, but would they take them out of the desert or deeper into their ruins?

"Does Kye know what he is doing?"

"He is scouting," Lightning hissed back, his eyes watching Kye's every cautious move.

As they watched, Kye began to turn on the spot. As he turned towards them, Rose saw that his eyes were closed.

"What is he doing?"

"Scanning for something," Lightning answered, glancing around him.

"Scanning! How can he do that with his eyes closed?"

"He's using magic," Lightning whispered.

Looking again, Rose saw that his face was creased in concentration.

She was about to ask Lightning what Kye was scanning for when Eloo's voice began to chant beside her. Rose glanced at her, to see that the small woman had her eyes closed and she, too, was turning on the spot. As Eloo turned in Rose's direction she felt something brush her awareness. It was like a butterfly fluttering at the edge of her consciousness and then it was gone.

"What was that?" she asked, breathless.

"I think Eloo is searching for thoughts," Lightning said, absent mindedly rubbing his temples.

Rose was still watching Kye. As she watched, he knelt down and his body shimmered, as if she was watching him through smoke or water that was disturbed.

"What just happened?"

Lightning opened his mouth to answer, but before he could all hell broke out.

THE WOLF HELM

"Goblins are our dark kin. They are the scum of our people."
The Elf records.

He watched the cursed, black maned werewolf move closer. Soon it would be in range, just a few more steps. The time was now. The orc hiding beneath the arch hurled its spear at the tall werewolf. The barbed head of the spear flew smoothly into its chest, but no blood flew from the wound. Instead, the werewolf's form shattered and then it was gone. The orc stared in disbelief, then snarled in pain as a black feathered arrow slammed into his shoulder.

The dammed werewolf was now standing a few feet left of where he had appeared to be. The orc roared as it broke the arrow shaft. With a bellowed command, it unsheathed a huge axe from its back and flung itself at this black maned foe.

Rose and Lightning however, did not have time to see this, they had their own problems. One moment everything was silent and still, the next the sky was raining javelins and arrows.

"Rose, take cover," Lightning said, and flung himself on top of her and bore her to the ground.

Rose was about to tell Lightning to get off her when a dart slammed into the ground next to her head.

"Cover your ears," Lightning hissed in her ear.

Rose did as he ordered and a second later a roar of sound that shook the ground beneath her told her he was using the wand that fired sonic energy. A high pitched squeal signalled something had been hit and a second later a body fell, landing just before her eyes. Rose blinked, and for a terrible moment she saw her father's stricken body, his white robe sprouting red roses on its once white field.

Then she shook her head and when she looked again, she saw that it was not her father, but one of their attackers. Rose realised her mind had played a trick on her and she groaned and felt a dagger of grief stab through her heart.

She shook her head, trying to clear it of these wild emotions. This was neither the place nor the time to grieve, she was in the middle of a battle for the god's sake. She bit her lip and driving back the tears and fears, stared at the body that was not her father's. As she watched, the thing that had fallen sat up and stared back at her. Rose flinched, taking in the elongated human features, the over large pointed front teeth, the yellow eyes and the long rat like ears that were bleeding. The rat like humanoid snarled and shook a short, jagged sword at her.

Rose reached for her sword, but she knew she would never get to it before the creature got her. Then a long form screamed over her to land on the rat-man, and Rose watched with amazement as Lightning hacked at the rat-man with his short sword. Struggling to her knees she was about to go to Lightning's help when she saw something that froze her in place. A long, jet black sword appeared from nowhere and hung in the air, as though it was being held by an invisible hand. Even as the idea sank into Rose's mind this black blade struck at Silver Skin.

The blow knocked from her hand the Wand of Wisdom, which she had pulled from her sash. It flew from Silver's hand to fall at Rose's side. Without even thinking about it, Rose grabbed the long staff and holding it up before her, watched as the rings began to revolve into new combinations. As soon as they stopped, Rose read the word that had been formed by the runes: "Ocula Verita."

Rose did not know what the words meant or even if she was saying them right, until she felt the energy well up in her and the world changed.

One moment Rose did not understand what, if anything, the magic had done, the next realised that it had changed her. She could now see that someone was wielding the blade. Rose screamed with rage, and ripping her sword from its back sheath she hurled herself at the figure in the black wolf sculpted helmet. This monster was the thing that had killed her father and she was going to settle that account now.

Kye saw the great, broad form of the man tall orc coming at him, its axe swinging. Kye fired another arrow at it and then cast his bow aside, but even as he did so he was fighting the orc. As he was drawing his short sword his left hand shot out to punch the orc's leather breastplate, with such speed that the orc never saw his hand move. It did, however, hear the wolf like cry that Kye unleashed as he launched the punch. It also felt the force of the blow, as it connected with its body and sent it staggering back several steps. In all its years no one had managed to land such a blow, let alone stagger it. This lit a rage in its heart that flared like a sun and it roared as it bodily launched itself at Kye.

But the tall werewolf was more nimble than he appeared and he easily leapt aside, avoiding the orc's wild swing. Then he grabbed hold of the orc's axe haft and stabbed his sword into the monster's body. The orc roared and drove Kye back with its shield. Kye staggered as the orc let him have the axe, sweeping out its scimitar.

Kye tossed the axe into the air, flipping it, so that it fell end over end and as it fell he caught hold of the axe haft and with all his strength behind it, struck at the orc's neck. Even as the monster's blade sliced across Kye's chest the axe cleaved through the beast's neck and the orc fell dead at Kye's feet, its head all but severed from its body.

Kye did not take time to savour his victory, for more of the short rat eared goblins were boiling out of the arch, their high cries filling the air. Kye grabbed his bow back up and began to pick off goblin after goblin. He fell back, retreating towards the others, but as he did he heard Rose cry out and glancing over his shoulder, he saw her, sword in hand, lunging at a too familiar sword.

"Kain," Kye snarled, his eyes flashing yellow as his anger boiled up.

Rose did not take time to wonder how she could see the Wolf helmeted killer. She knew on a subconscious level that the magic was allowing her, and he must be invisible. Nor did she take in that he was, although revealed to her, still clothed in a shimmering dark cloud. No, she took in none of these details, she would do that later.

At the moment, all she knew was that this was her father's killer and she was going to kill him. She drew her sword and flung herself at him.

He became aware of her and the fact that she could see him. As Rose rushed at him, he danced back from Silver who was blocking his sword with her staff. Rose swung at the helmed head, but he easily blocked her attack and countered, sliding his sword under Rose's and thrusting it at her throat.

Rose, however, was still clutching the wand and she stabbed its point at one of the eye holes of the mask, from which a pair of yellow eyes glowed. As she did this she spat more magic words at the black armoured figure. Where these words came from Rose had no idea, for they sprang into her mind from nowhere and she was not reading them off the staff. One moment her mind was a vengeance storm of anger, the next, words of golden fire were emblazoned across her inner eyes.

As Rose cried the words, there was a flash of red light and the black armoured form was sent flying backwards, as if it had been plucked up and flung by a huge, invisible hand. Rose herself was flung to the ground from the backlash. She glanced around her, her world suddenly foggy, as if she was seeing through a mist.

Lightning's and Silver's voices came to her from a distance as if she was hearing them through water. Then everything went dark. Rose waved her hand before her face, feeling that she was still awake, but the air around her was as dark as pitch. Had she gone blind?

"Rose, speak to me!" Lightning's voice was suddenly clearer, as if the fog had cleared from her ears, but she could still not see.

"Lightning, why is it dark?"

"Kain has used the Fang of Void to summon a cloud of darkness, don't move."

"But what about the goblins? They love the dark."

Lightning did not have to reply to this, for seconds later the curtain of night was torn aside by a brilliant blue light that burnt through the darkness. When Rose's eyes cleared it was to see the horde of goblins cowering back from a wall of flickering blue flames.

These flames gave off a cold light and Rose could feel their icy breath, which Silver was creating judging by the way she was gesturing with her staff.

"What is that?"

"Ice fire," Lightning said, gently helping Rose to her feet, handing back her sword which had been knocked from her hand when she cast the magic.

"Will it keep those things back?"

"They are not likely to break through it," Lightning said, and fired his crossbow at one of the rat-men. "But Silver cannot keep it up forever. When it fails the goblins will attack."

"Those things, they are goblins?"

"Yes, but you already knew that."

"I suppose I did. I thought they didn't like the daylight?"

"If you look carefully, you will see they are still sheltered by Kain's cloud of darkness."

Squinting against the bright dancing flames that radiated not heat but cold, she saw that above and around the Rat forms there was a cloud of inky darkness that swirled and moved as if disturbed by invisible winds.

"So what do we do?"

"Retreat, I suppose."

"Where's Kye?"

Kye appeared next to Silver, his bow singing as he sent an arrow through the wall of flames.

"Silver, we have to leave, the fire will not keep them back long."

"If we could only break Kain's darkness," Eloo snarled, and launched a bolt of energy into the boiling sea of grey bodies.

"Your wish is my command," Silver said, through gritted teeth. Grasping her medallion and raising her eyes and staff to the heavens, she called down power from her goddess.

"Silver Lady I call upon your illuminating light, please light our darkest hour."

For a long time nothing happened and Rose thought Silver's plea would not be answered, but then a silver light poured down from the heavens. It was as though a full moon had come from behind a veil of clouds to light the square in the middle of the day. The dark cloud that swirled around the horde of goblins was burnt away as the wall of blue flames flickered out. The goblins screamed, quailing at the light, and turned tail and ran into the dark arch, the last three falling to the werewolves arrows.

"Well done, Silver," Kye said, and helped her up from where she had sunk, spent, to her knees. "However, this is not a victory, for they will be back at nightfall."

"And in greater numbers, if our luck holds," Lea muttered.

"Then we had better get out of this cursed place before then, hadn't we?" Eloo said, examining the cut in Kye's tunic.

"It's fine, E, he cut the cloth, that's all."

"What about the rest of you?" Eloo said, eyeing each of them and searching for wounds.

"What about you, Rose, how do you feel?"

"Like I'm dead on my feet," Rose said, leaning on Lightning's arm.

"You used the Wand to see Kain?"

"Yes, Lightning, but what I can't understand is where the other spell came from."

"You mean you cast a force field spell without the use of the Wand?" Silver asked, her voice sounding strained and hoarse.

"I guess so," Rose said, and flicked her gaze from Silver's drawn face to the many strange runes on the Wand. "What is happening to me?"

"We will figure this out, Rose," Lightning said softly, as if he was speaking only to her. "I promise you that."

"We don't have time for this now," Lor said, glancing at the dark arch.

"Eloo, Lightning, do either of you have the strength for a light spell?"

"What do you have in mind, Kye?"

Kye took one of his arrows and held it out to Eloo, who gave him a bright if tired smile, as she touched its glittering tip and half closing her eyes muttered a few words beneath her breath. Kye gently removed the arrow from her hand and turning, sent the missile flying into the dark archway. The arch was suddenly lit by a dazzling bright light that showed creeping grey forms screaming and falling in shock to the ground.

"As I feared. They are gathering for another assault."

"They were waiting for us?"

"Yes, Lor, but I fear not us specifically."

"The Moot."

"I agree, Kye. Kain has taken charge of a horde of goblins to ambush anyone coming for the Moot."

"The nations will have to be warned."

"I will see what I can do," Silver said, and she closed her eyes and her brow wrinkled, as if she were concentrating hard.

"Which way do we go now?" Eloo asked, and blew on the end of her wand.

Kye looked at the two other roads that led out of the square. He glanced at Silver and she shook her head. Kye turned to the east, leading them out of the square and amongst taller and taller ruins.

Soon the sky was just a blue ribbon, a ribbon that was getting darker. A ribbon that showed just how little time they had left to escape this maze.

After the company left the square and the dust had settled, a long shadow fell across the man sized orc and the iron shod foot of a staff touched its forehead. A voice that chilled the air it passed through filled the silence with its deadly whisper.

"In the name of the dark powers I summon your soul back to this body, so that you may serve our need."

A dark mist spiralled out of the air and entered the orc's staring yellow eyes. A cold light lit them and he drew in a rattling breath through his healing throat.

THE GREEN GATES

"The lands of the Elves are defended by more than the Silver Shield's bows."
Silver Skin, the Wereding Chronicles.

The way they were taking led them ever east and Rose was beginning to suspect Kye was lost in this maze.

"Lightning, where are we going?"

"Out of here, I hope," Lightning said, and made her drink some mouthfuls from his water skin.

"Thanks," she said, and handed the skin back, but as she did Lightning grabbed and held her hand.

"Lightning, what are you doing?"

Lightning did not respond, staring at her hand, which he eventually released. "Tell me, Rose, how long have you had that red mark on your hand?"

"What red mark?"

Rose lifted her hand to the level of her eyes and examined her hand, but saw nothing different.

"The back of your hand."

Rose turned her hand and gasped to see a large patch of her skin had turned a bright red. She stared at this patch of raised, scaly skin. "What is this, Lightning?" she whispered, staring with horror at this change.

For a moment Lightning did not answer, but instead gently took her hand again and lifting it close to his face, studied the hardened skin.

"I am not sure, Rose," he said, letting her hand drop, his face frowning. "I have not seen anything quite like this before, well I have and I haven't."

"What do you mean?"

"Eloo I need you to look at something for me," Lightning said, though his eyes never left Rose's worried ones.

"What is it L?" Eloo asked, and bounded up to them.

"Rose, show Eloo your hand," Lightning requested.

Rose hesitated, but held it out to Eloo.

Eloo whistled and reached out a finger to touch the hard, scaly skin. "Can you feel me?"

To her surprise, Rose could feel Eloo's gentle touch through the scaly skin. It was true that some feeling was lost. She could not feel Eloo's breath like touch as well as when it passed over her unaffected skin, but when Eloo touched the scale, Rose knew it.

"Yes, I can."

"What if I do this?"

Rose was about to ask what, when from Eloo's fingertip there sprang a long claw, which Eloo stabbed into the scale.

"Ouch," Rose said, feeling a dull pain penetrate through the scale. Rose snatched her hand back. "That hurts!"

"Not as much as it hurts me," Eloo said, holding up the finger, to reveal to Rose that the slender claw had broken off at the tip.

"So what does that prove?"

"It proves that you still have touch, but the skin is now armoured."

"But what is it?"

"Does it remind you of anything, Lightning?"

"Actually, I was about to ask you that. Fire Drake skin."

"What are you saying?"

"Nothing, really, all we are saying is that it looks like the scales of a Fire Drake."

Rose stared from Eloo to Lightning, not believing what she was hearing.

"Are you telling me I'm turning into a dragon?"

Expressions of surprise flashed across the two faces.

"Actually, that wasn't what we're saying."

"Then what are you saying, am I dying?"

"Please Rose, calm down," Eloo said, touching her arm. "I do not believe you are dying. Why would you think that?"

"There is a disease that corrupts the skin and wastes the flesh, they call it cancer."

"Ah, I see, well there is an easy way to settle that one. If Silver feels up to it she can find out if you are ill."

"I can," Silver said, and limped up beside them, leaning heavily on her staff. "But I must rest first. I am still spent."

"Can we afford to rest in this place?"

"Perhaps not," Silver said, her eyes trained on where Kye was standing, his head low to the ground at a T-junction. "But I must rest if I am to be of help."

"Is something wrong, Kye?" Eloo asked, skipping to his side.

"This path takes us north...but there is a scent here I do not like."

"So what do we do? The night is coming, and we can't stay out in the open with goblins about."

"There is a place here we could hide in," Lor suggested, and glided towards a low doorway.

"Wait," Kye ordered. "You do not know what is beyond the door, let me go first."

Kye, an arrow leading the way, pushed past Lor and standing at the doorway he cast about, then disappeared into the darkness beyond the low doorway.

"Kye, is everything all right?" Eloo asked, hovering at Lor's side, staring into the dark with her faintly glowing eyes.

After what seemed an eternity, like an echo of the past, Kye's voice reached out to them from the darkness.

"Come in, it's safe enough."

Eloo did not need any more invitation, she flew into the dark. Lor shrugged and followed them.

"Into the heart of Darkness," Silver said cryptically, and one by one they entered the darkness.

By the time Rose entered the low room, there was a ball of cold blue light hanging in mid-air which showed her they were standing in a low ceiling room barely large enough for the whole of the party.

"Well, this is cosy," she said, watching Lightning conjure a fire from nowhere. "Won't the goblins find us here?"

"Not once I get to work," Eloo said from the corner of the room, where she sat cross-legged, her eyes closed.

Rose watched, as Eloo began to rock gently. Her hands wrapped around a medallion, which glowed between her fingers. Eloo's lips began to move as she formed strange words and a sudden breeze stirred the dust at the door entrance. Eloo rose with her animal grace and proceeded to dance around the room and to Rose's amazement, she never touched one of the party. This was even more a miracle, for she had her eyes closed. Rose spun on the spot to follow Eloo as she danced round her, the chant rising like the wind that now swirled the dust so that it filled the low doorway. As Rose looked back out into the outside world, she realised that it was slowly becoming dimmer, as if she were seeing it through a thickening mist. Then the doorway had gone, disappearing behind an almost impenetrable wall of darkened glass or thick fog.

"It should hide the entrance from normal eyes, even those of a goblin," Eloo sighed, and fell exhausted into Kye's arms.

"We still post a guard," Silver said.

"Lightning, yours is the first watch," Kye ordered, as he fed Eloo from his water bottle.

Lightning nodded and filling a pipe, sat in front of the door, taking out his wand to lie beside him.

Rose walked across to where Silver sat, her eyes closed, her head back against the wall. For a moment Rose wondered if she was asleep, until Silver spoke.

"You want me to check you for disease?"

"Please, but if you're too tired..."

Silver gave a long sigh and opened her eyes. "I am tired, but if you give me a moment I will do as you wish. If you are prepared to accept the truth."

Rose gulped, realising what Silver meant. Did she really want to know if she was dying? Could she face that knowledge?

"Well, are you?" Silver asked, her glance suddenly piercing.

Rose could not endure that glance, so she turned away from the Druidess to study the fire, to find to her surprise that she was gazing across the fire and into Lightning's eyes. He quickly turned his head back to the doorway, but Rose realised he had been listening and she felt, though she could not say why, that he was encouraging her to go ahead. Was he, and if so, why? She knew he was a friend, but was there something more in that glance?

"Rose?"

"Yes, I am prepared for the truth. Whatever it is."

"Then sit before me," Silver said, and reached for her silver pendant.

Rose sat cross-legged before the Druidess, who drew from her belt pouch a small leather bag. From this bag she poured a small pile of dark brownish dust or rust, Rose wasn't sure. She began to chant, stirring this dust with one hand while the silver medallion glinted from between the fingers of the other hand. As she chanted, the dust crumbled and disappeared as if it had never existed. The silver disk that the Druidess held began to radiate a bright silver light that shone through her fingers. Rose saw that Silver's eyes, too, were beginning to glow with the same light, as if a moon had been placed inside her skull. Even as Rose realised this, Silver opened her eyes wide and Rose had to blink, as a bright silver light reached out to flicker across her face. As she blinked, she felt a cool touch on her face and sweep over her body. When she had stopped blinking, it was to see Silver's eyes returning to their normal yellow shade, a gentle, if tired smile crinkling her lips.

"Well, tell me the worst," Rose whispered, her voice suddenly robbed of strength.

Silver's smile widened and Rose was not sure what that meant. "It is exactly what I thought. I found what I expected to find."

"Well, am I infected?"

"Only with an incurable desire to ask every question that pops into your head," Silver said, her whole personality beaming at Rose. "Rose, you are a perfectly healthy young lady. A little tired, a little hungry, but apart from that there is nothing wrong with you."

Rose could not speak for a long time, as relief washed over her and she was surprised when tears fell onto her hands in her lap.

"Rose, why are you crying?" Eloo asked, surprised at her reaction. "If you had anything wrong with you, we could quite easily cure you. We have healers who can heal anything."

The relief, however, was short lived as she realised that although this was good news, it did not answer another important question. "But if there is nothing wrong with me, what is this?" she asked, holding out her hand before her so Silver could see the dark scaly skin.

Silver sighed, and took Rose's hand, gently stroking the changed skin. "I am sorry, Rose, but I don't have an answer."

"Could it have something to do with the magic she cast?"

"I don't know, Eloo, but that is an idea, an idea I will have to sleep on."

"But you all wield magic, don't you know how it works?"

"We do use magic," Silver said, her eyes going distant. "But magic is a subtle thing. It can have unforeseen results and it has its own rules, and only our greatest sages understand how it works."

"Is there anyone who might know?"

"Great Mother or one of the other Druid council. Once we get to the Moot we can ask. All I can tell you at the moment Rose, is that you are not diseased or cursed, so get some food down you and get some rest and take one day at a time."

Rose pulled her hand from Silver's and turning away, gave vent to her emotions, as tears welled up and poured down her face. She wiped her eyes on the sleeve of her jacket and moving across to a spot near Lightning, she sat and tried to take in what Silver had told her.

It was fine for Silver to tell her to just accept this change, she didn't have to look at her knuckles and see them bright red. She became aware that someone was watching her and glancing up from the scale, she saw Lightning.

He smiled as their eyes met. "Try to get some sleep," he said gently. "I find that everything looks better in the morning."

Rose shrugged, but stretching out, she lay her head on Lightning's pack and before she knew it, she was snoring gently. Only once he was sure she was asleep did Lightning move across to where Silver was watching Rose sleep.

"Did you see something else?"

"No," Silver said, hesitantly.

"But you know something about this?"

"It is a suspicion," Silver said slowly, as if she did not want to tell him. "I think Rose has magic in her blood, this is why she can cast magic without teaching."

"Like an elf?"

"Not quite, Lightning, elves and werewolves are beings of magic, we are able to access magic that is part of our spirits, but we still have to learn the necessary words. We must still study and practise. We must learn over years how to use our powers, but Rose seems to be able to cast without learning. She cast a forceshield, a magic that usually takes several years to learn, but she knew what the words were. She did not even need the magical materials to cast such a spell. She cast using her blood."

"But that is how dragons cast magic. They can reach into their race memories and find the necessary words and gestures, so how is Rose able to do this?"

"Lightning," Eloo, who had been listening closely interrupted. "Have you never heard about the Sparks among your people?"

"You think Rose is the offspring of a Fire Drake?" Lightning asked, taken aback by this idea. "But if she is why doesn't she know it and why doesn't she display the signs of dragon blood?"

"I thought you would have the answers to those questions, Lightning," Silver said pointedly.

"I will have to think on this."

"Would you be able to ask your mother or her family about this?"

"I am not sure. I am not sure that I want them to know yet."

"Then you are falling for her," Silver said, smiling.

"Does anything escape you, Silver?"

"Not much. So are you going to tell her and if so, what will you tell her about yourself? Will you reveal what you really are?"

"I do not know Silver. I have no answer to your questions."

"Well, it is your affair, Lightning, but if you would take my advice, I would tell her soon and I would tell her the truth."

"You would! Is that wise?"

"Possibly not, Lightning, but it is what I would advise."

"Well, I will have to think on that too."

"Think all you want, but I wouldn't think for too long, or she may find out on her own and that definitely would not be good."

Rose found herself in a grey mist. A mist that surrounded her on all sides and obscured the ground. It was as though she was in the middle of a cloud. Suddenly the mist parted to reveal another cloud. A jet black thunderhead of a cloud, that swirled and twisted in a pillar to form a humanoid figure. A human figure that stared at Rose with flaming red eyes, that burnt into Rose's soul and she felt they would burn her up, but when she thought she could not endure the heat any more the mist rolled back across the scene, obscuring the baleful cloud and shielding her from the heat of that gaze. Rose cowered down like a rabbit, feeling the cloud come closer and although she could not see it, she could feel its presence close at hand.

"Please, please don't let it find me, don't let it find—."

"Rose, Rose, wake, you're having a nightmare."

Rose woke, to find Lea shaking her shoulder.

"Where is it?"

"Where is what, Rose?"

"The dark cloud," Rose muttered, and blinking, she realised where she was.

"If you mean the weather, it hasn't changed since yesterday, but it is dawn and we need to be moving, so rise and shine."

Rose sat up, to see Lor spreading out several arrows on the ground, splitting them into three piles and sliding them into the three arrow bags. She noticed there weren't many to go around.

"We have used up most of them, fighting the drake and fending off the goblins," Lea said, noticing her glance.

"Will there be enough?"

"Enough to see us through the next step," he answered, giving her a reassuring smile that did not quite convince Rose.

Rose turned to the fire, where Eloo was boiling a kettle.

"Let me guess, more porridge?"

"Give that girl a gold star," Eloo said, grinning at her. "But don't worry, we're nearly home and when we are I'll give you a feast that will make these rations taste like dirt."

"Have you ever eaten dirt?"

"I've eaten your cooking, Lightning," Eloo shot back, serving up the porridge.

Rose realised that one of the company was missing. "Where's Kye?"

"He went out before dawn, to scout," Eloo said, her grin disappearing as she was reminded of the concern for her lover.

Her concern was soon removed, as Kye appeared at her side to lift a spoonful of the thick liquid from her bowl.

"Speak of the devil," Eloo said, her face breaking into a huge grin. "How lies the land?"

"Rocky," Kye said, and took a long pull on his water skin.

"Why, what's wrong?"

"The road leads to the north and may come out near The Gate of Fawns."

"So what's the problem?"

"The problem, Lea," Kye said, gruffly, "is that there is an obstacle in our path."

"What kind of obstacle?"

"Some of the ruins have slid and there is a considerable landslide to get around."

"Passable?"

"I think so."

"Did you not climb it?"

"Yes, but as a wolf," Kye answered.

"Then that is a problem."

"Did you follow past the slide?"

"Only a little way, from the scent the goblins patrol that ground regularly. I did not want to alert them to my presence."

"How do we proceed?"

"We go forward," Silver said, and rinsed her bowl out with water and stowed it in her pack.

Kye picked up his reloaded arrow bag, bow and pack and led them out of the room that had been their home for a night. They turned left as they left the room and Rose blinked on entering the grey light of day. She was hustled along by Lea while she blinked and when she had recovered, she found herself rushing along another featureless road. Then the high buildings that had fenced them disappeared and the sky opened up to show grey clouds as far as she could see. She gazed around her, to see why. The ruins that had stood several storeys high must have been small structures here, for although their remains were still around they made much smaller heaps, though one of them had spilled its walls right in their path.

This meant that for what seemed like miles around there were hills of rubble. Directly in front of them, where the road would have continued was the lowest pile of rubble, but it was still a tall climb, that stood more than ten feet high.

"What's on the other side, Kye?" Rose asked, eying the hill of unstable bricks and twisted metal.

"A continuation of the road, but it is higher on the other side, so it is easier to get down."

"Like so many things, it is easier to get down than up," Lightning said, grinning at Rose as he tested the ground before him with his walking stick.

"It's also easier to fall than stand," Rose said, but she followed Lightning closely.

"Keep on the left," Kye said from his position in front, he too using his bow like a staff to test the solidity of the ground before him.

Rose glanced past Lightning, to where Kye was for a moment

silhouetted against the sky before he disappeared from sight.

"What's happened to Kye?"

"It's fine, Rose," Lightning said. "He has just gone over the crest and you can't see him from this angle, that's all."

"Kye, how does it look?" Eloo asked, leaping like a mountain goat past them and to the heap's crest.

Kye did not respond, but there was a scuffling sound from beyond the rubble.

"Kye, is everything all right?" Eloo asked and then she gave a cry and vanished too.

"Eloo, what's going on?"

"It's fine," Eloo answered, after a pause. "Kye and I are fine."

"For now," came Kye's bitter response.

"What's that mean?"

"It means that a goblin scout has got away from us."

"Are you hurt?"

"No, but he got away to tell the rest of the rats where we are."

"It's morning! What is it doing out here in the light of day?"

"That doesn't matter at the moment," Silver said, as she too reached the heap's crest. "How long do we have, do you think?"

"If they are prepared to chase us in the day maybe an hour," came Kye's grim response.

"How far to the gate?"

"I am not sure, but unless there is any obstruction larger than this between us and the gate two, three hours."

"It's going to be close," Lightning said, as he reached the top and turned to help Rose.

Rose took his hand and just as she did lost her footing, so that she was suddenly hanging in mid-air. The only thing stopping her from falling was Lightning's hand, but to her amazement Lightning easily lifted her through the air, to place her on her feet beside him.

"Just how strong are you?" she asked, leaning on his arm.

"Strong enough to keep you safe," Lightning said, staring deeply into her eyes.

Rose blushed and turning away, looked around her. She could see miles of crumbling ruins, but when she turned northwards she could see that the ruins stretched for only a mile or less and then a huge wall loomed up. This wall was not grey but dark green and brown.

"What is that, Lightning?"

"That is the wall of the north watch, a great hedge that keeps the Grey Desert out of the elf woods."

"It's huge!"

"It has to be, but it's no wall of China," Lea said from behind her.

"The wall of where?"

"It doesn't matter," Lea said, nudging Lightning. "If you've finished sightseeing, do you think you could move on?"

Rose followed Lightning down the other side of the slide, to find that Kye had been right. The heap was smaller on the other side, or the road had been higher on this side. Whatever the reason, the route down was over before Rose knew it and they were back on the road again. Rose saw that the buildings were little more than waist high here and she could see that the road led almost straight towards the green wall. She turned to speak to Lightning, when Lor, who was the last to traverse the heap, gave a cry and tumbled down to land at their feet, an arrow protruding from his shoulder.

"Lor, are you all right?" Lea asked, and pulled his brother to his feet.

Lor did not answer, but yanked out the bloodless arrow and lifting it to his mouth, licked the point.

"Apart from being stuck with goblin rubbish, fine," Lor said, and broke the arrow over his knee.

"If they are risking pot-shots, they can't be far away," Kye said as he restrung his bow.

"How long?" Silver asked, drawing a long dagger from her sash.

"Ten minutes," Kye said, and began to lope along the cracked road, his long legs striding out as he increased the pace.

They began to move more quickly and Rose checked around her, feeling they were being watched by unfriendly eyes. As they passed under a high wall a short figure leapt down in front of Kye, a long handled axe held above its head, its yellow eyes glaring at the werewolf and its long fangs bared in a snarl.

Kye, however, did not hesitate, even though the creature was only a foot in front of him. He drew and released his bow in one smooth action and shot the attacker at point blank range. The arrow hit the creature in its forehead and even as it stumbled back, Eloo danced forwards to spear it on her sword.

"An orc of the Euric tribe."

Rose moved up to stand beside Kye to stare at the attacker. It was a short figure, about Eloo's size, but broader and stocky. Its skin was a bright yellow with black veins running through its body. Rose noticed that its head reminded her of a dog's, its nose almost merging into a muzzle with its fangs protruding from under its snarled top lip. It was dressed in a leather breastplate and kilt. The stench that came off the thing's body was like nothing she had ever smelt before. The long black hair that covered its head and flowed to above its yellow eyes was filthy and matted.

"So that's an orc?"

"Yes, and where there's one there's bound to be ten more," Kye said, kicking the orc's body.

Trying to ignore the orc's stench, Rose regarded the short dogman who already seemed to be rotting before her eyes, or was that her nose?

"But I thought goblins and orcs didn't like daylight?"

"And this one wouldn't either, but he's wearing this," Eloo said, holding up a ring of dark metal.

"A Ring of Shadows," Silver said, taking the ring from Eloo. "That explains a lot."

"And it raises more questions at the same time," Lightning said, loading his crossbow.

"Yes, but here is not the place to ask them," Kye said and led them on.

They were soon among small ruins, and as they topped a rise in the road, Rose saw that the road dropped to a short plain only a bow shot to the great wall of green hedge.

"We're home and dry."

"Not yet," Lea said. "Behind us!"

Rose turned to see hundreds of grey forms boiling out of the ruins on every side, their weapons glinting blackly through the dark mist that hung about them.

"Everyone move," Lea said, pushing Lightning forward, as a dozen arrows fell around them.

"Run," Kye shouted, and picked Eloo up, slinging her over a shoulder as he loped down the hill to hit the plain running. Silver was just behind him and Lightning and Rose found themselves running shoulder to shoulder. Lea and Lor stayed only a moment, to lose an arrow at the approaching horde, before they, too, took to their heels.

Rose was in good shape despite her shoulder wound which was nearly healed, but she could not keep up this pace.

"How much further?"

"We're nearly there," Lightning said, glancing over his shoulder.

Rose looked past Silver to see the great green wall, but to her dismay, she could see no break in it. How would they get through it? How could they escape the screaming mob on their tail?

"Kye, where's the gate?" Lea called from behind as he stopped to shoot another arrow at the screaming mob only yards behind them.

"We are feet from it," Kye said, scanning. "This way."

He led them to the right and as they moved along the green wall Rose saw the mob moving to flank them. She watched as one of the large yellow creatures stopped to glare at her and cocking its arm it aimed a javelin at her. Rose braced herself for the strike but it never came, for Lightning's crossbow vibrated and the orc fell, a bolt in its throat.

"They're getting closer," Lightning said as he reloaded his bow.

Rose, who realised she had just had a brush with death, could not speak, but she nodded as they followed Kye along the wall that was now sprouting six inch long thorns gleaming wickedly in the dew of morning.

The orcs, perhaps knowing their destination and planning to prevent them, flung a cordon in front of them. More might have joined this thin line if they had not been outside the cloud of darkness.

Still, half a dozen large orcs stood before them. Kye shrugged Eloo off, shot two orcs before they knew what had happened and then drawing his short sword, let loose a wolf like cry and charged straight through the line leaving dead orcs in his wake. Eloo followed him, dancing around the slower orcs, slashing open the backs of legs and leaving orcs screaming and thrashing on the ground, immobilised.

Silver, following their example, smote an orc with her staff and stabbed her dagger into the face of another. Rose ran after them.

Thankfully, the others had dealt with most of the orcs, but she still had to slam her shield into a tottering orc before she was free of the picket.

She was wondering where the gate was, when she knew she had reached it. The green wall suddenly parted, to reveal a high arch that stood twice the height of a man and was constructed of the entwined branches and trunks of two huge trees that grew to form a narrow arch. Rose was still running when she realised the arch was beside her and might have gone past, if Kye's long arm had not shot out to grab her shoulder and yank her through the portal to land in a heap at his feet. Rose lay there gasping, until a thought occurred to her.

She had thought this arch would have gates they could close against the orcs, but this gate was an open arch with neither gate nor door to close. Lightning, Lor and Lea tumbled through the arch and took up defensive positions.

"Silver," Rose gasped, between intakes of breath. "How...do...we keep 'em out?"

"The land of the elves isn't protected by bows alone," Silver said, and laid her hands on the tree trunk that formed the arch.

Rose realised the trunks were exquisitely carved, with runes and magical symbols that were beginning to glow with a blue light.

"Lea, step back," Kye said, as the younger werewolf began to strum his bow.

He did as Kye ordered and as he stepped back from between the trunks, a curtain of filmy light fell between them and the outside, so that a veil seemed to have been drawn across the doorway of the arch.

"It's magic?" Rose asked, feeling a warm glow emanating from the arch.

"A very old and powerful warding magic," Kye said, and shot an arrow through the veil.

"Will it keep them out?"

Kye might have answered her, but he did not have to, as a particularly large orc hurled itself at the curtain. As it hit it turned red and bounced off the door, falling to its knees screaming, as its flesh smoked and blackened.

"It would appear so," Kye said, putting an arrow through the wounded orc's throat.

"What about them shooting through?"

"We are about to find out," Silver said, watching a company of goblin archers draw and loose a cloud of arrows at the arch.

Rose could not help but crouch behind her shield as the arrows flew towards them, and she flinched when they struck the door and fell harmlessly to the ground.

"Any more questions?"

"Yes, can they get through with that?"

The thing Rose was referring to was a dozen orcs carrying a bulk of wood that may have been a tree trunk and which they were preparing to use as a battering-ram.

"Can the arch withstand a battering-ram?"

"Lea, Lor, draw back," Silver said.

The two werewolves did as ordered, but continued to make the music of war with their bows, their arrows picking off some of the ram bearers, but the ram continued to forge forwards.

"Don't worry, Rose," Silver said, grinning. "The arch looks after itself."

As the ram came within a yard of the arch, the hedge on either side came alive and attacked the orcs. Rose watched with disbelief as long vines and branches reached out to wrap around the orcs, lifting them and flinging them high into the air. Others, the living arms of the arch impaled on long thorns and tore at the orcs yellow flesh. Rose gasped as she saw one orc gripped by opposite branches and spatter its blood against the curtain as it was bodily torn in half.

Rose shuddered to see this, but whereas she was shocked by the bloodshed, the rest of the company was pleased by it. Eloo whooped with joy as the blood sprayed against the veil. The twins pounded their bows against the ground, as they too yelled at the sight of the orcs defeat. Silver grinned broadly and even Kye's mask cracked a little, as his lips twitched.

Lightning seemed pleased with the results. However, he sensed her disgust. "We are safe, Rose," he said and sank to one knee, his energy flooding out of him.

Rose still shuddered, staring out at the now bloody ground, but Lightning was correct. The orcs were drawing back. A few angry archers shot a last defiant volley, but they were not even in range and fell spent yards short. Lea watched them fall and was about to dart out for them, when Kye, sensing his thought, lay a heavy hand on his younger brother's shoulder.

"Don't even think it," he growled.

"But they're just lying there, we could refill our bags."

"It is outside the veil," Kye said, his eyes burning into his brother's.

Lea shrugged and turned away from the curtain. Even as he did the glowing veil flickered and died out completely.

"It's gone!" Rose said, suddenly afraid that the orcs, if they realised it, could come back and get through the gate to pursue them further.

"Don't worry, Rose," Silver said, sheathing her long knife. "The veil activates in the presence of evil, and it has gone because the orcs have gone."

"But they could come through this way once we're gone, couldn't they?"

"No, the barrier is only visible when orcs or other evil is around, but the wards that protect this gate are always active; the veil is only a visible effect of the magic. Please believe me, we are safe now. We are in the Elven Woods."

THE FOREST OF THE ELVES

"The woods of the Elves is a place alive with magic. Even the trees have a mind of their own."
Eloo, the Wereding Chronicles.

R ose gazed about her, to see the gate they were standing in was only part of the huge green wall. The hedge must run back ten feet before it stopped. They were standing in a green tunnel made of interlinked branches which led them out into a short grassy meadow running in either direction as far as Rose could see. However, directly in front of them was another dark wall. One of the trees towered higher than any Rose had ever seen. Unlike the hedge, these trees were not a solid barrier and were more like the pillars of a great building than the walls of a fortress. Rose was about to ask the party what the trees were, when a movement at the corner of her eye distracted her. She stared towards the huge roots, to see several figures emerging from the trees.

"Are they really what they appear to be?"

"Yes, Rose," Lightning said, his voice full of amusement. "They are Centaurs."

Rose watched as about a dozen of the giant creatures galloped towards the party. They must have stood seven feet tall and had the stature of giants. It was not their statuesque human bodies that held her amazed stare, but the glossy horse bodies that grew from their waists. She had always thought they would look odd, but they were so graceful and beautiful. As they drew near, long lances lowered as if for a charge, she drew back in fear. However, they did not attack, but drew up in perfect formation. A move that was even more impressive because not an order had been given. One moment they were pounding towards the group, their hooves making the ground tremble, the next they had come to a stop, forming two lines about six feet apart. They held their lances at an angle to form an arch of honour.

The leader of this company, a Centaur with long, almost white blond hair and the body of a palomino, who wore a helmet mounted by a wolf's tail and bearing a blue shield with a silver sickle moon, bowed to Kye and spoke to him in a tongue Rose did not recognise.

"It is fine, Fist, Rose is a friend, you may speak openly before her and in the common speech."

The Centaur bowed and spoke again in a deep voice. "As you command, my commander..."

"How many times, just Kye."

The Centaur nodded and began again. "Kye, I and the blades of the south patrol are glad to see you safe."

"The pleasure is all mine," Kye said, smiling broadly and stepping forward to place a hand on the tall Centaur's shoulder. "It is always an honour and pleasure to see you and your brothers."

Kye turned from the Centaurs and looked at Rose, his smile no smaller. "Rose, may I present Windfist and his brothers in the Silver Guard."

"Honoured, I'm sure," Rose said, when she finally found her voice.

The Centaur bowed and studied her face with a pair of very blue eyes. His look was open and Rose, although she did not feel like she did when the werewolves did this, still felt that this being was seeing part of her she did not necessarily want him to see. She blushed and found herself looking down to see that the Centaur was wearing a breastplate over chainmail. Around his waist he wore several heavy leather shields that guarded the horse body's chest and the tops of its forelegs.

These thoughts were interrupted by Eloo's velvety voice purring. "You will have to forgive her, Fist," Eloo said. "You are the first Centaur she has seen."

Windfist saluted Eloo with his drawn scimitar and bowed low to her as he replied, "I see, Your Highness, I am glad to see you safe with us again."

Rose, who was a little overwhelmed by the size of this strange creature, was not too overwhelmed to notice that he referred to Eloo as 'Your Highness'. Why was this Centaur referring to Eloo as if she was royalty?

Eloo frowned at this, but returned Fist's salute with her rod. "Fist how long have you been on watch?"

"Lady Silver Skin," Fist said, saluting again, "I have been here for the last two days."

THE AWAKENING OF MAGIC

"And you know about the Moot?"

"We have been ordered to watch out for all pilgrims."

"Have any of the pack come through yet?"

"Unfortunately, not to my knowledge."

Silver exchanged a glance with Kye at this news.

"Fist, are you and the Shield aware that a large goblin horde is attacking anyone who travels through the Desert?"

The Centaur snorted, as an expression of shock passed across his face. "I have not heard of this, my Lord."

"We were ambushed in there and so will anyone else coming that way. The word must be spread."

"Fire Feet," Windfist called out to the ranks of his Centaurs.

From their ranks there sprinted what she at first thought to be a foal or a child on a pony, but when it came to rest before its officer Rose saw that it was a very young Centaur.

This child of the Centaurs was tiny, coming up to Fist's hip or perhaps Rose's waist, but she, for it was a girl with breasts like any woman, had long black hair and several raven's feathers braided into her dark locks. Despite her childlike appearance, she was clad in studded leather and bore a short bow and a brace of long knives serving her as short swords. She must have felt Rose's eyes on her, for she scanned Rose, but returned her attention to her officer, when he snorted.

"Captain," she acknowledged, in a high sweet voice, though it was more the voice of a woman than a girl.

"Take a message to headquarters that goblins are prowling the Desert. The nations must go around, not through the Desert."

"It is done, Uncle." Even as these words passed her lips, she spun on the spot and was gone in a blink.

Rose blinked, not believing that the tiny horse-girl had disappeared, looked around and, spotting a flash of black against the roots in the distance, stared at the distant trees and realised that it must be the messenger.

"Good god, she's fast!"

"The fastest in our patrol," Windfist said proudly.

"How old is she?"

"Fire Feet is in her twentieth summer," Windfist said, sheathing his sword.

"She's a little short, isn't she?" Rose said hesitantly, not sure how he would take this.

Kye threw back his head and barked out a laugh. "There you are again Rose, asking the embarrassing question."

Fist watched this, a curious expression on his face, but he answered Rose's question when she looked to see if he had been offended.

"Fire Feet is a Dwarf Centaur. Her branch of the family is descended from a sub branch of our race. Nevertheless, she is one of the fastest scouts we have. If you would step this way, we would be honoured if you would take a meal with us."

As Silver opened her mouth to respond, somewhere behind them a high, clear bell chimed.

"What's that?" Rose asked.

"The gate bell," Windfist said, cocking his head. "Someone is coming through."

Silver closed her eyes and laughed. "It is Great Mother and Flash."

Kye and Rose spun to face back towards the gate, to see emerging from the green tunnel two huge figures and behind them many, many other smaller figures. Rose had not seen the two werewolves in their human form, but she recognised them nevertheless. They were still giants, for the male, who must be Flash was over six feet tall and as broad as a barn door. He wore only a kilt and a baldric across his back for the huge long sword in his hand. Beside him was a silver haired woman who must be Great Mother, dressed in a brown robe. She was carrying a gnarled staff in one hand and a scimitar in the other. Rose noticed both blades were stained with blood and Great Mother's robe was also splashed with blood.

"Goblins?"

Flash did not answer, but nodded to Kye's question. It would seem Flash was as closemouthed as his son.

"Lord Flash, what are your orders?" Windfist had gone down on one knee, his head bowed almost to the ground.

"Rise," Flash said, in a voice that seemed to come out of the earth itself. "Has the Shield been warned?"

"A message has just been sent."

"Then a pack must be gathered to secure the run, but for now, food and drink," Great Mother said in a gentle voice that for some reason made Rose think of running water.

"This way, my lady," Fist said, rising and leading them through the guard of honour's arch of lances.

Rose's group stood to one side as Great Mother and Flash went before them through the arch. Rose watched the rest of the large party passing. She saw a strange menagerie of beings.

"Witness the Elven nations in a snapshot," Lightning whispered in her ear.

Rose watched, as creature after creature passed before her, each one seeming stranger than the last. Directly behind Great Mother and Flash there came a handful, or should that be pawful, of the huge werewolves, their yellow eyes baleful, their presence made all the more threatening by the blood staining their muzzles and paws. One of the huge creatures was still chewing on something that Rose did not want to see more closely. On the backs of the last few werewolves were several small creatures, clinging to the long hairs of the wolves or to each other. They were small men and women, some nearly as tall as Eloo, but most were much smaller. Some were only a few inches tall.

"Dwarfs," Lightning said, then pointing to a group of figures that were only a foot in height or length, said, "Gnomes."

These gnomes were not what she had expected. They were human in appearance, but their skin was brown and almost muddy, like earth, and their long hair was green and resembled moss or creepers. Following the werewolves was a couple of what appeared to be giant lizards. One of them, a bright red one, crept up to Kye and stared at him with its huge lidless eyes. Rose was surprised to see Kye bend and say something softly to the lizard thing, which stared up at him and stuck out a large, forked tongue to receive a biscuit, which it vacuumed into its huge mouth. Rose watched its large throat moving as Kye stroked its spike ridged back. As Rose watched, the lizard's skin slowly faded from bright fiery red to become a soft green.

"Go, Skin Speaker, go and re-join your fellows," Kye said, to the lizard, which hopped off.

"What was that, apart from what it looked like?"

"Skin Speaker, one of the Chameleon-men," Lightning said, as he smiled after the Chameleon-man. "He is a shy thing, but Kye seems to have a soft spot for him."

"He is one of the Silver Claws," Lea said, overhearing.

"He has served the Shield well for many years, but he is still a little shy."

"The Silver Claws, what are they?" Rose asked, watching a chestnut Centaur trot past, leading several of her daughters.

"The Shield and the Elven army has many branches, and the Silver Claws are our spies and assassination squads," Lea explained, saluting the Centaur woman who returned his salute with a long sword that still had a stain of blood on it.

Rose was about to ask something else, when Eloo gave a cry and bounded forwards to embrace the next figure. This figure was a tall woman, who had long green hair that fell to her waist and who was wearing a dress that appeared to have been made from grass or weaved plants. Her skin was the brown tint of wood. She flung her long arms round Eloo and although she draped her arms over the little woman, she had to look down on her.

"Father," this woman said, in a soft whispery voice.

"Willow Skin," Kye said and had to wipe a tear away from his cheek. "I am glad to see you."

With this, he wrapped the two women in his long arms.

"Who is that?"

"Willow Skin, Eloo and Kye's daughter."

Rose looked back at this tall woman with increased interest as Eloo led her towards the group. The two women were talking animatedly in a high tone that was so fast Rose could not even make out single syllables, let alone words, while Kye trailed them, his eyes never leaving his daughter. Rose watched them draw nearer as a grey bear led a fleet of pack horses past, their backs laden with everything you could think of.

"Rose, come meet my daughter, Willow Skin," Eloo enthused, her face glowing with pride and love.

Rose stepped forward and extended a hand to the tall, willowy woman, who took it and studied Rose's face with a pair of eyes that were like deep green pools. Her hand was smooth, but her long fingers wrapped firmly around her hand. When she spoke, her voice was a whisper that conjured to her mind the image of a wind whispering through leaves.

"Pleased to meet you," she said, and a broad smile lit up her face which reminded Rose of Eloo.

"Likewise."

"Hello, Willow," Lea said, stepping forward and giving her a huge hug. "So tell us, what's been happening?"

"Ah, Uncle Lea, it is good to see you again," she whispered, though it was a whisper that carried and Rose could hear it even over the loud squawking of several bird like people passing them. "I heard the call and on my way through the Birches came across Grandmother and Grandfather and came with them."

"The Centaurs are waiting," Lor pointed out, as the rest of Flash's party had passed through the honour guard.

They passed under the arch of lances and moved slowly towards the trees. The Centaurs waited until they had all passed and then began to follow them, some overtaking them and passing on either side, disappearing into the trees before them.

"Willow, you still haven't told us what happened in the desert," Lea prompted.

"We were passing through, having gathered up more of our party along the way, when we were ambushed by an unusually large group of goblins."

"But you aren't hurt, are you?" Eloo asked suddenly, carefully studying her daughter.

Willow extended her left arm, to show a long scratch on her smooth, if bark like skin.

"Stop fussing, E," Kye growled at a fussing Eloo. "She's fine."

"The goblins," Lea persisted.

"Grandmother summoned a great elemental and Grandfather used the Silver Death to beat them back and we broke their back."

"How many did they kill?" Lea asked, as if he wanted to make notes.

"Don't worry, Lea," Lor said, nudging his brother. "Willow can give you all the gory details for your Bardic records later. Let's get some food in us first."

"Yes, I could do with some water myself."

They slowly drew nearer to the trees and as they did Rose watched, as more mysteries of the elves unfolded before her. The trees were huge, towering up into the air, their long shadows reaching out to embrace anyone approaching. However, Rose did not notice that. What she did notice were the huge mushrooms that clustered around the enormous roots rising out of the ground, like strange animals waiting to greet the new arrivals. On these mushrooms squatted many odd creatures, among them several of the lizards that were the chameleon-men. As they drew near the huge trunks, Centaurs appeared to guide them between two pillar like tree trunks and further into the trees. The sun disappeared as they entered under the great canopy, though it was not entirely dark, for light did filter down through the green roof. Rose heard a strange bird call and looking up, saw on a huge branch a massive bird. Its wings spread to more than fifteen feet, though what was more surprising, was the small figure mounted on its back.

"Wing," Lightning shouted up to it. "What is the news?"

"The Moot is gathering," came back a high pitched voice, and the bird took flight.

"Where are we going?"

"To the guard house, I think," Lightning replied.

"And what is that?"

"That," Lightning replied, pointing to a small opening in the trees before them.

They broke into sunlight, to find themselves in a small clearing in the trees and before them towered what must have been a huge stump. Atop this trunk stood a Centaur guard, his bow aimed in their direction. The centaur guiding them raised his lance and gave a signal as he dropped it in a particular way. Rose, gazing around, saw that all the members of Flash's party were spread out around them in the clearing.

"Water?" a centaur asked, stepping up with bowls of spring water.

Rose took the bowl and took a long draught. It was the coldest and best drink she had ever had.

"That's good," she said, handing the bowl back to the waiting centaur.

"No, thank you," Willow said, as the centaur offered her the water. "I would rather drink from the spring itself."

The Centaur bowed and moved on to Eloo, who splashed some of it on her face before drinking.

"What of the gathering? Has any force been gathered to clean out the goblins?"

"I believe that Lord Flash has gone onto headquarters to organise that," the centaur replied. "You may rest."

"We saw a messenger."

"Yes, a wing is scouting out the desert."

"Damn, I wanted to pass on a message."

"Fire Feet may have returned by now, Lord Lightning."

"Good, if she has, send her to me, would you."

"What's the rush, L?"

"The rush, Lor, is that I wish to contact Takana," Lightning said, handing the Centaur a small cake of some brown substance.

"Thank you, Lord," the Centaur said and bowing turned away.

"What was that you gave him?"

"Tea," Lightning said grinning. "They don't always get supplies out here and it always pays to pay the piper."

"Tea," Eloo said, grinning herself. "Yes, tea would be nice."

Rose opened her mouth to reply, when the world around her swirled and disappeared, as she was engulfed by a dark mist. Rose felt the world falling away, and the mists surround her like a shroud. Then she saw them, the red fiery eyes glared at her out of the mist and Rose felt beams of heat scanning for her, but for some reason they could not find her. She felt their heat pass and re-pass, but still the blazing eyes could not find her.

Rose came back to herself, to find Willow Skin bending over her.

"Where am I?" Rose asked in a slurred voice, for she realised she was lying down.

"You collapsed, so we have put you in this bower."

"Are you all right, Rose?" Lightning asked, propping her up and giving her a mug of what turned out to be hot and sweet tea.

"I think so, I feel dizzy."

"Just rest for a moment," whispered the tall form of Willow Skin.

"What happened?"

"We were hoping you could tell us," Lightning said, and tried to smile at her.

Rose suddenly remembered the flaming eyes that had been searching for her.

"It was the eyes again," she muttered to herself.

"Eyes?" Lightning asked, catching her mumbled words. "What eyes, Rose?"

"I had a dream, well more a nightmare, in the ruins. This figure with glowing red eyes was searching for me. I saw it again just now."

"Rose, listen, this is very important," Lightning said, his face coming close to hers. "Did this figure find you?"

"No... at least I don't think so... I'm not sure. But Lightning, what is it?"

Lightning sat back on his heels and looked across Rose, to where Willow Skin was kneeling. Her eyes were far away, as if she was not hearing them. When she spoke, her voice came from a distance. "I can sense no sensor, but they may have stopped."

"Lightning, please tell me what's happening to me."

"Nothing is happening to you... well it is, but it's not what's happening to you that's the problem. Damn, I'm not explaining this very well." Lightning took a moment to take a deep breath before he continued. "Someone is trying to scry for you and you, for some reason that is beyond me, are able to sense it."

"Who would be scrying for me?"

"That's a question I can't answer," Lightning said, looking to Willow Skin for help.

She, however, did not appear to have any better idea than he did, or at least if she did, she was not letting on.

"Why would they be scrying for me?"

"That is what we would all like to know," Silver Skin said, appearing behind Willow Skin. "It would appear that we are not the only people interested in you."

"Silver, can you help?"

Silver cocked her head as she considered the question. "Perhaps I can," she said speculatively.

"Can you help, Silver?"

"I can and I can't," Silver said, fingering her silver pendant. "I cannot discover who is scrying for you, unless I detect it in progress, but I might be able to protect you from the scryer."

"How?"

"It would involve magic, Rose," Silver said.

Rose, who was still reluctant to have anything to do with magic gulped, but nodded in spite of herself. "What kind of magic?"

"It is a kind of veil, or screen," Silver said slowly, as if her words were not adequately describing it.

"When will you do this?"

"Not now, I am afraid, Lightning." Rose's disappointment must have shown because Silver clarified, "I need some rest before I do such a magic and we need to move on to the Moot."

"Only if Rose feels up to travelling," Lightning insisted.

"How is she feeling?" Eloo asked, popping up beside Willow Skin.

"Fine, I think," Rose said, and taking Eloo's outstretched hand slowly got to her feet, where she stood swaying.

"Small steps," Lightning said, supporting her on the other side.

"This is becoming a habit," she muttered.

Kye appeared before them, one of the wooden water bowls in his hands. He held it out to her and Rose gratefully took and knocked back the cold water. The cold, sharp spring water was like a burst of strength.

"Thanks, Kye, that's just what I needed."

"I thought it would be," Kye grunted. "Ready to go on?"

"I think so."

Kye smiled slightly and then turning led her across the clearing, to where half a dozen horses waited for them. "I thought they would help carry us quicker to the Moot."

"They probably will, but could someone give me a jump up? I'm too tired to try."

Kye lifted her and placed her on the horse's back. It was only once she was there that she realised there were no reins. "How do I stay on?"

"Grasp the mane," Eloo advised, as Kye lifted her, too, onto the back of a horse. "But not too tight, he won't thank you for that."

"Here, Rose, let me help you," Lightning said, and climbed up behind her, his arms reaching around her to grip the horse's neck.

Rose felt immediately safe and reassured.

"Thanks, L."

"Are we all ready?" Kye asked from beside the head of Eloo's horse.

"Lead on, Kye," Silver said, atop a large grey.

Kye, who had not mounted a horse, whispered something in Eloo's horse's ear and the horse snorted and trotted at his side as he led them to the tree line. They were about to enter the trees again when Kye stopped and held up his hand, as if he had realised something, or as if he had noticed something. As Rose's horse swayed to a stop, a high, strange cry came out of the trees in front of them. A cry that made the horses whinny and Lightning had to say something to the horse to get it under control. The cry was that of a bird, Rose thought, though she could not have said what kind of bird. It reminded her of a hawk. Then the owner of the cry emerged from the trees and Rose gasped, as a creature out of myth stepped out.

It was huge, probably ten feet from beak to tail. It had the body of a Lion, but its head was that of a massive bird of prey, an eagle? From its shoulders there sprouted the largest pair of wings Rose had ever seen on anything, save perhaps the Fire Drake.

"Is that what I think it is?"

"Yes Rose, that is a Gryphon," Lightning whispered in her ear.

Kye gestured for the horses to move back, to allow this new creature more room and as they watched the cat thing stalk past, Rose saw that it too had a rider. Seated on its back and strapped into a high saddle was a tall female form. Rose only got a glance of the woman, but what she saw convinced her that the Elven lands must breed goddesses, for this woman could have been forged from living bronze.

"Who... what was that?"

"An Amazon of the Golden Winged, our cavalry," Silver said, watching the figure pass, its double curved bow lifted to acknowledge Silver's salute.

As they watched, the huge cat made an enormous leap onto the high tree trunk and from there into the air, the wings unfurling and flattening the grass as they beat down in a thunderclap, to lift the Gryphon and its rider high into the air and over the tree tops, to disappear against the blue sky.

"Where is she going?"

"Probably to hunt goblins," Lightning said, as Kye took charge of them again and they returned to the woods.

For a long time they moved through the woods and Rose's world became dappled light and dark shade. She was almost dozing when she realised they were no longer alone. There were others in the woods with them. She looked about her, to see a huge, grey form pass her like a stone ghost in the murk. Rose stared after the form of a giant man that could have been carved from stone.

"Lightning, am I dreaming or did a statue just walk past?"

"Oh Rose, you are a wit," Lightning chuckled in her ear. "In a manner of speaking, yes. It was a troll, an earth elemental."

"I've heard of them, but I didn't realise they grew that big."

"I must admit, that was the largest I have seen in a long time, but the call of the Moot draws all our people. Even waking trolls."

"And trees," Willow Skin added, riding past them and tapping one of the huge trunks.

"What does she mean?"

"I'm not quite sure," Lightning muttered, his gaze going between her and back at the tree.

Rose glanced around and once she thought Kye and Eloo were out of earshot, she asked Lightning a question in a quiet voice.

"Lightning, is Willow Skin a werewolf or an elf?"

"In a way, she is both and neither," Lightning answered her in an equally quiet voice.

"Then what is she?"

"That is a harder question to answer," Lightning said, with a sigh, then after a pause to let a dark shaggy bear pass, he continued. "We are not as obsessive with naming everything as you humans. If Willow Skin did have a racial name, I suppose Dryad would be the closest description for what she is."

A Dryad. Rose had heard of these ancient beings too. They came out of the mists of time and were supposed to be the spirits of the trees. Yes, the green haired woman with her smooth bark like skin did resemble a tree spirit.

"But why is she like this and not an elf?"

"You are delving into deep waters here, Rose."

"Sorry," Rose said, blushing as she realised she might be asking things she shouldn't.

"You don't need to apologise. I don't mind being asked or even answering any question, but there are questions I do not have the answers to."

"And this is one of them?"

"Yes and no. It is not that I can't answer you. It is that I do not know how to explain the answer, as I understand it."

"Please try."

"Very well. It is all to do with our natures. Eloo is an air spirit, whereas Kye is a werewolf and is, therefore, closer to water. So their child is a merging of those natures and magics. Willow is the element of wood and is a merging of water and air."

Rose thought about that and said what came to her lips, without her bidding it. "That does and doesn't make sense."

Rose started, as a deep rich laughter seemed to come out of the earth itself and found that Willow Skin was riding next to them and had overheard the whole conversation.

"She expects the workings of magic to make sense!"

Rose looked at the tall woman, to see if she had been offended, but Willow simply grinned at her.

"Rose I am sorry, I am not laughing at you, so much as at the idea of magic working as you seem to think it should. As you learn more about magic, you will learn that it is chaotic and works to its own rules and whims."

"I am not sure that I do want to learn any more about magic," Rose whispered to herself, staring at the scale on the back of her hand.

Willow Skin, however, must have very good hearing, for she heard Rose's mutter. "If I am any judge, Rose, I think you cannot escape magic or its workings."

Rose opened her mouth to ask her what she meant, when the horse whinnied and her attention was drawn to what was before them. The trees had been thinning and now disappeared completely and before them was a broad trench that must have been eight feet wide and which, like a moat, stretched before them, cutting them off from the opposite bank. On the other side of that trench were high wooden towers, like a castle drawbridge, though if so they had been left behind and the rest of the fortress had been moved, for they stood alone, and alongside them there grew more of the great trees.

"What is this, another defensive wall?"

"Yes, but it was originally a canal," Lightning said. "This is one of the ways across."

"We could get down into it, though."

"Have you seen how steep the sides are? Besides, look more closely."

Rose did and saw that the trench was filled with strange bushes and vines, all with wickedly long thorns and strangling vines that moved and writhed, as if they were alive and only waiting to strangle and impale anything foolish enough to enter their domain.

"I must be asleep, but they feel like they're alive."

"Of course they are. All plants are living creatures," Willow Skin said. "But if, as I perceive you mean, they are intelligent, you are correct. The magic has made them more and they would kill you if you fell in."

Rose shivered, imagining what it would be like to fall into that writhing nest of poisonous plants. Then her attention was distracted as a grating sound filled the clearing, and looking up she saw a large drawbridge descending to span the gap. As this bridge lowered, Rose could see through the widening arch two huge statue like trolls working the chains. Kye led Eloo's reluctant horse onto the planks and through the arch.

Rose wondered if she could make herself cross the trench, but before she knew it, Lightning had dug his heels into the horse's flanks and the bridge was booming closed behind them. Rose watched as the huge statues released the massive chains and stared at her with coal black eyes. Silver said something to them in a grating voice and placed in one of the troll's massive paws a scroll of dark parchment.

"This is a toll bridge," Lightning explained. "You pay what you can, but magic is most useful to the door warders."

"Where do we go now?"

"There is a small belt of trees and then we are there."

"Where?"

"Care Diff, our capital city and the seat of the Sylvan Throne."

"And can we rest there? I feel like we've been travelling for weeks."

"Yes, Rose, there we can rest."

"The wardens will guide us from here," Kye said, indicating a waiting figure.

This, what Rose took to be a young troll, was a statue like figure of a boy and although his skin resembled marble, the eyes were a clear blue that stared at Rose with the same curiosity she was giving him.

"This is Steelgar," Kye introduced him, and bowing, he laid his bow in the stone boy's hand.

"Thank you, Lord Kye," the stone youth said in response, his voice surprisingly soft, if raspy, reminding her of the chink of pebbles.

"Kye giving his bow to Steelgar is a ritual," Lightning explained, as the stone boy led them through the trees. "By giving his bow up, Kye gives over his guide role to Steelgar."

"And he's taking us to this Care Diff?"

"He is."

"What is it like?"

"Your eyes can tell you better than I. Look."

As Lightning said this, the trees vanished and they came out on the banks of a large lake. Mirrored in that dark water were hundreds of lights. Rose gazed up from the lake, to see on the other side of the water a huge hill that rose up before them, its trees filled with lights. As Rose stared she realised that many of the huge trees were laced with tall stone towers, like those of a castle, and she realised that whether tree or tower, a huge city towered above her. A city that must be as large as Landon.

"That's your city?"

"That's Care Diff, the heart of the Elven Kingdom."

Rose stared at the city, overwhelmed by its size. "I never knew there were so many of you."

"Rose, you have missed the point, we have been trying to tell you. Our people are older than man, and we have never left these lands. When men dwindled, we grew. Now we number in the thousands. Come, we will show you the strength of our people."

MOONSTONE'S NEWS

"Prophecies are like riddles written in an ancient language. You have to interpret them and even then the translation may lead you astray."
Kye, from the Book of the Wolf.

Rose half expected another drawbridge or a ferry to take them across the large lake, but Lightning said, "No." He explained that the waters were sacred and the nations did not cross, but passed it to their city.

"Only the inhabitants of the lake may cross it," he said, watching Kye, Silver and the rest genuflect at the water's edge.

"Should we do so?" Rose wondered, though she noticed that Lightning was watching only.

"I am fire, not water," Lightning said, interpreting the question on her face.

"You do not worship our gods and powers, Rose, we do not expect non-believers to follow our customs," Willow Skin said, rising from a kneeling position.

The stone boy led them to the west and they skirted the lake by following an avenue of trees. Willows, Rose thought, but she was not sure in the dimming light. What she did notice was that the trees were interspersed by large standing stones that bracketed the path they were taking, and although it was reminiscent of the ruins, Rose did not feel afraid here, as she had in the ruins. If anything, she felt at peace, as though she was making for her home after a long day. In fact, she had almost nodded off when Lightning nudged her.

"Hey, sleepy head, don't you want to see Care Diff up close?"

Rose lifted her heavy head and gasped, as the hill now towered above her. From the other side of the lake it had appeared huge, but now when she was under its very eaves, it seemed to fill the world with its tall stone walls topped with glittering spikes. Beyond that a ring of trees rose up to the pinnacle of the hill, itself crowned by a tree so huge and wide that Rose wondered how it did not collapse under its own weight. However, she only took in these details later. What she noticed at once were the lights. From the wall topping spikes to the highest branches, the city hill was glowing with lights of every imaginable colour and shape. Candles glowed in the tall towers arched windows, red and gold lanterns hung in the tree branches, and in the very air there floated tiny lights that darted to and fro, as if they were blown by the wind.

"What do you think of it?" Lightning asked, a little apprehensively, as if he half thought that Rose would hate it.

"It's beautiful," she breathed, for she was almost speechless in her overwhelming love of the hill. "What are the floating lights?"

"Fey," Lightning said as if this was the most normal thing in the world.

"What do you mean?"

"They are fey, tiny fairy kin. You'll see. But now is not the time to explain, we must prepare for the guard."

"Guard?"

"Weapons may not enter the city. We must leave them with the guard."

"What, even my father's sword?"

"Even that. Don't worry, Rose, they will give you a receipt and look after it. I promise."

"But I mean your people no harm."

"I know that, and you know that, but they don't. Please don't make a fuss about it. If you don't want to enter the city we can remain outside and still attend the Moot, but if you want to see the city and all its wonders, you will have to submit your father's sword to their care. Look, even Kye is giving up his precious black bow. Now if he can do it, surely you can."

Rose was not so sure, but realising they were approaching the entrance to this hill city she craned her neck to see the gateway. The entrance appeared to be a pair of gates wrought of a jet black metal that stood closed before them and which was guarded by two of the largest men Rose had ever seen. They must have stood twelve feet tall and wielded maces six feet in length.

"Are they Giants?"

"Yes, the gates of the Metal Veil are guarded by the Iron guard," Lightning replied, watching Kye and Eloo give up their weapons, all but Eloo's wand.

"Why aren't they taking her wand? Isn't that a weapon?"

"Yes, but it is also a proof of Eloo's rank and a ceremonial tool. But watch this, they are about to pass through the gates."

Rose watched, as one of the Giants blew a note on a huge flute and Kye and Eloo passed between the huge guards and approached the still closed gates.

"The gates aren't opening for them!"

"These gates do not open," Lightning said, laughing as he watched Rose's reaction.

Lightning was right, the gates did not open, but they did let Eloo and Kye through. As the two approached the huge metal bars, they vanished. One instant the gates were there, as solid and immovable as a mountain, and the next they had vanished like a morning mist.

Then, as the two lovers passed through the white stone, the black gates reappeared to bar the way to any the Giants would not allow entrance.

"Is it an illusion?"

"I doubt it," Lightning said, and passed over his crossbow, short sword and a dagger. "Come, Rose, give the sword up."

Rose reluctantly and slowly unbuckled her scabbard and held it out to the huge Giant, who broke his mask of a face with a large smile as he received the sword.

"It will be safe with us, lady," he said in a booming voice that sounded like thunder, or an avalanche heard from a distance.

"Please do," Rose said, watching the other giant write up their receipt and hand it over to Lightning, who stowed it in his pack.

"Please pass through," the Giant who had smiled at Rose said, while his colleague blew his flute.

"Come, Rose, let's go through."

But Rose hesitated, staring at the walls, realising that beyond was a world of mysteries and magic. What would she find? What secrets would she discover? Most importantly, what would she learn about herself?

Lightning placed a hand on her shoulder and steered her towards the gate.

"Please, Lightning, let go," Rose said, staring at the gates.

Lightning did as she asked, but placed it round her shoulder. "Is this all right?"

"Yes."

"Then come, let's go through."

They walked towards the gates and as they drew close, they vanished and Rose could see a long tunnel with a pair of large double doors at the end. Once they had passed under the arch and into the tunnel, Rose glanced back to see that the large bars had reappeared and looked as permanent as they ever had. They walked along the long tunnel, made of the white stone of the wall, but at intervals there were niches in the wall and as they walked she glanced into them and started when she saw what rested there.

"Bones!"

"Sorry, what was that, Rose?"

"Lightning, why are there bones in the niches?"

Lightning stopped and glanced where she pointed. "Oh, I had forgotten about those."

"Why are they there?"

"They are the remains of past guards, who died in service of the gates. They are put in the recesses so that their spirits will watch over and guard the walls."

"It's ghoulish," Rose muttered.

"Perhaps, but it is with the guards' consent."

"Hey, you two, move along, you're holding up the rest of us," Lea said from behind them.

Lightning, still with his arm round her shoulders, continued to lead her to the doors.

"Are these gates magically closed, too?"

"Only in times of war or when the city is under siege," Lightning said, and gave one of the doors a gentle push so it easily and silently swung outwards.

They emerged through the doors to find themselves in a wide opening, like a square, a feeling that was emphasised by the fact that opposite them was a pair of tall, castellated towers. However, although this square had a small fountain in the centre of the area, it was grass and turf and not stone, and was more a field than a square.

Lightning took his arm from around Rose's shoulders and Rose felt bereft as he did so. Why did she feel disturbed when he moved his arm?

From beside the fountain Eloo waved at them, but there was no sign of Kye.

"Where's Kye gone?" Lightning asked, as they strode up to her.

"He's gone to see what is being done about the goblins."

"Does that man know when to rest?"

"Probably, he thinks he knows everything else," Eloo said grinning. "But for my part, I could sleep for a week."

"I will drink to that," Lea said, and dipped a jack into the fountain, drinking deeply from it.

"Can we rest now?" Rose asked, yawning hugely.

"Yes, we can rest now," Lightning said, grinning equally hugely.

"These are the towers of rest," Eloo said, pointing to the towers that were lit from within by a soft light that illuminated without being too harsh on the eye. "Step this way."

Eloo led the party to the nearest tower where they were met by two women dressed in white robes, their hair shaved close to their heads. They reminded Rose of priests.

"These are Sisters of the Church of Peace," Lightning whispered.

"We come in peace," Eloo said, smiling at the sisters.

"Then go in peace and enter in and rest," the sisters said in soft voices.

The sisters led them through a low door, into a hall lit by a soft, blue light that came from the stone walls themselves. In the middle of the hall there stood a trestle table, laden with plates of food and cups of water.

"Please eat, drink and refresh yourselves."

The party descended on the tables like a swarm of locusts. Once they had done justice to the food and drink the Sisters took them through a low door and into a long low dormitory lined with beds, many of them already occupied. Rose was directed to a bed and not bothering to pull off her clothes she fell onto it, and closing her eyes fell into a deep and untroubled sleep.

When Rose came round, it was to find the dorm empty and a bowl of water standing at her bedside. She bathed her face and walking through to the dining room found Lightning and Eloo eating.

"Good morning," Rose said, sitting on a low stool opposite them.

"Good afternoon," Eloo shot back, grinning round a roll.

"How late is it?"

"About ten," Lightning answered, pushing a plate of cheese and cold bacon towards her.

"Thanks, what are those?"

Rose was pointing to where Eloo was nibbling on a kind of pancake or filled wrap.

"This?" Eloo asked in surprise, lifting the pancake towards Rose, who saw that a string of melted cheese was hanging from it.

"Well blow me down! You haven't seen an oatcake before?"

"No, if that is an oatcake, then I haven't seen one before. You wrapped your cheese in it?"

"And bacon, and sausages and egg and pretty much everything I can," Eloo enthused.

"I have never heard of them."

"That might be because they tend to be a local delicacy and have been for hundreds of years," Lightning said, as he showed Rose that he was wrapping his bacon in the pancake. "Or at least Kye tells that they were eaten in these parts long before the great burning."

"Can I tempt you?"

Rose considered the wrap and shook her head.

"I'll pass today and try another time, thanks. This morning I'll stick with rolls."

"You don't know what you're missing," Eloo said, and filled another oatcake.

"Thanks, but no thanks."

"Good, all the more for me," Lightning said, and took a huge bite of his bulging oatcake.

"So what happens now?"

"As with everything, Rose, that is up to you," Eloo said, as she pushed her plate away and drew towards her a parchment of some kind, and dipping a quill into ink she began to write. "We will attend the Sylvan Throne, but you do not have to. You could stay here or wait for us outside the city. Your fate is your own."

Rose chewed slowly, considering what Eloo said. If she stayed behind she would see none of the wonders or learn any of the answers to the questions she kept asking herself.

"I would like to attend the Moot, if it is permitted."

"Why wouldn't it be?"

"Because, I am not one of you, am I?"

Rose watched closely, as Lightning and Eloo exchanged a quick look.

"Well, am I?"

"You are not an elf, it is true," Eloo said thoughtfully. "But you are an elf friend, so you are welcome to attend the Moot."

"An elf friend, does that mean I am a member of the club?"

Both Lightning and Eloo laughed at that.

"I think that yes, you are a member."

There was a murmur of voices outside and then a knock came and a head of tousled, raven locks peeked nervously round the door.

"Moonstone!" cried Eloo, who springing to her feet, bounded to the door and drew a small and wiry girl in grey robes through the door.

"Hello, Aunt Eloo," the girl piped, her bright blue eyes shy and hooded.

"Rose, let me present Moonstone, Kye's youngest and loveliest sister."

"Pleased to meet you," Rose said, smiling at the girl, enchanted by the girl's meekness.

"She is also out of school," said Kye's voice from the doorway.

"I have been summoned by Mother," Moonstone said in a tiny voice.

"I know it, M," Kye said softly, turning the girl around to face him. After he looked her up and down, he wrapped her in a warm embrace. "It has been too long."

The girl did not answer him, but buried her face in his chest and whispered something into his brown tunic. Kye growled something back and then holding her at arm's length looked her full in the face.

"You have news for me?"

"I was asked to study the writings of the Grey Pilgrim," Moonstone squeaked.

"And what did you find?"

Moonstone did not answer, but fumbling at her waist she drew from a belt bag a scroll. She handed it to Kye, who unwrapped it then stared at it.

"What makes you think that this is the necessary writing?"

"There are many volumes of his writings," Moonstone whispered. "But when I opened the storage bin that holds them, this one was lying open on top."

"That is not enough."

"No, it isn't, but as I cast my eyes on the page a Moon Moth alighted on it and with its proboscis touched the first line of that text."

Kye grunted in acknowledgement, accepting this as reason enough, and stared once again at the parchment.

"A Moon Moth?"

"Have you never seen one?" Eloo said smiling. "They're a rare moth said to be servants of the Silver Lady. They give off a glow like moonlight and are considered omens by werewolves and the Lady's followers."

"So, what does it say, Kye?" Lightning asked. "Or are we not permitted to know."

Kye did not for a long moment answer Lightning. Rose guessed he was considering whether to tell them or not. Then he read the scroll aloud. "When the Silver Lady is imprisoned, her people will be crushed. Unless the cleaved mirror is mended, they will be lost."

"That doesn't sound good," Rose said.

"Was there any more?" Eloo asked, prowling round the room.

"He goes on to say that the Sylvan must pass into the mist if they are to survive."

"None of it makes any sense to me," Rose said.

"That doesn't surprise me," Eloo threw over her shoulder, and she turned away.

"What is that supposed to mean?"

"What I say," Eloo said, turning back to face Rose. "I am not surprised you do not understand the prophecies of a man who has been dead for over three hundred years."

"Well, do you know what it means?"

Eloo shrugged and picked up her scroll, packing it into a stone box.

"No, not most of it, but I bet Kye does."

Kye, who had been staring into the air before him, came back to them at the mention of his name.

"Well, Kye, what of it?" Lightning asked as he charged his pipe. "Do you understand the prophecy?"

Kye's eyes went to Moonstone and Rose, once again, thought an unspoken conversation was going on between the brother and sister.

Moonstone was not as expert at hiding her emotions, and she

seemed troubled, whereas Kye's face was masked. For a long time they debated a point with their eyes, then Moonstone made a small shake of her head and Kye turned abruptly away, as if he was disappointed by her response. Moonstone, for her part, appeared troubled and almost upset by this reaction.

"I have an idea what the last part of the message may mean," Kye said haltingly, as if he was not sure he should be telling them this. "However, I will have to consult Silver Skin before I can be sure."

"That means it is a Druid matter," Lightning muttered to Rose, and aloud to Kye, "Druid politics, Kye?"

Kye, however, was not there, he had vanished.

"How does he do that?" Rose asked for she had not even realised he had moved, let alone left the room. "Is it magic?"

"Once again, Rose, no, just skill," Eloo replied. "Moonstone, are you staying for the Moot or must you return to the Under Halls?"

"Unless I am told otherwise I will stay for the Moot," replied the girl meekly.

"Excellent! Then let's go and find out what's happening," Eloo said, suddenly a tiny dynamo.

"What about the others, shouldn't we wait for them?"

"They will catch us up," Eloo said, and gathered the three up and bustled them out of the door and along a narrow path that had been made by many feet beating the ground, rather than by stones being laid.

THE FAIRY LANDS

"Elves, what are they? To my way of thinking, the best place to find
their kind is in the tales of old, where they give you board and lodging,
but take your eyes in way of payment for their pies. Here they are
called fey and this is indeed the best way to name them. For although
they may not be evil, they can still be cold and cruel in their way. For
evil is a cruel, human concept, it has no place in a world of their rule!"
From the Wereding Chronicles by the Red Wizard.

L ooking in front of her, Rose saw that the next part of the city
was a ring of small buildings, interspersed with several towers.
These were dwarfed by the wall of trees that rose behind them.
"What are those trees? I've never seen any grow so tall."

"They were ordinary oaks and ashes," Eloo said, bounding along
at Rose's side. "But they have been infused with magic and have
grown so tall because they want to."

"That makes no sense," Rose said, wrinkling her brow. "Eloo, you
make it sound as if the trees were alive."

"But trees are alive, Rose."

"I know they are living things," Rose snapped, "but you make it
sound like they actually decided to grow, as if they think."

"And who says they don't?" asked the soft voice of Willow Skin
from behind them.

Turning, Rose saw the tall woman and her father had come up
silently and had been watching them while they stared at the city.

"You mean to tell me that trees have minds?"

"I mean to tell you that these trees may have minds," Willow Skin
corrected gently.

"Never mind that now," Eloo said, bouncing on the spot. "I want
to get to the Moot, come on."

Eloo bounded off in the direction of two large towers bracketing
the path they were on.

"She is eager, isn't she?"

"More so than usual," Kye admitted, smiling after her.

"Well, shall we join her?"

"By all means, lead on, Macduff," Kye said dryly.

"Who?"

Rose's question wiped Kye's smile off his face and he looked hurt.

"What did I say, am I supposed to know who that is?"

"No, Rose, probably not," Kye said, a sadness seeming to settle over him. "Please forgive me, I forget how much your people have forgotten about your culture."

"Then you should teach her, shouldn't you," Lightning said, as he followed Eloo towards the towers.

"What is it that I should know, Kye?"

"It does not matter now, Rose," Willow said gently, laying a gnarled hand on her shoulder. "Kye can teach you the play later. The Moot is close at hand."

Rose nodded, and with Kye on one side and Willow Skin on the other, she, too, moved towards the towers.

"Are these towers of peace?"

"No, they are guard posts," Willow said, pointing out an armed Centaur at a low door in one of the towers.

"Are all these buildings guard towers?"

"Most," Kye answered her, returning a Centaur's salute. "But there are barracks and private homes here."

"And beyond the trees, what part of the city is there?"

"The Temples of Art and War," Willow answered. "But most of the city is before that."

"Where, under the trees?"

"No Rose, in them," Willow corrected. "Many of the Sylvan live in the trees."

"What, up there?" Rose said shuddering, staring up the huge tree tops that must have been hundreds of feet above her. "I am not sure I could do that."

"And yet you have no trouble in our tree house."

"But that isn't so high off the ground."

"Everything is relative, Rose," Kye pointed out.

"Ah, the traders are cashing in on the Moot, I see," Willow Skin said, as they came to a wide space between the first ring of buildings and the next.

Rose looked about her, to find that a wide array of creatures had set up stalls, wagons, and seats and were hawking all kinds of things to the many Elvan travellers passing through the area.

"Is there usually a market here?"

"Yes, but it isn't normally this large," Lightning said, waving away one of the brown skinned gnomes.

"Mushrooms," called the gnome.

"No, thank you," Rose said, as the trader waved a tray of brightly coloured fungus under her nose.

The gnome might have persisted with Rose, but when he saw Willow Skin he turned away and rushed in the other direction.

"He went with his tail between his legs," Rose said, studying Willow Skin. "It was almost as if he was afraid of you, Willow."

"Well, let's say embarrassed," Willow Skin admitted. "I am... what did Lightning call me... a Dryad, and so he knows that I might take offence at him selling any green."

"Would you?"

"Probably not," Willow said shrugging. "After all, as long as some of the fruit is left to seed the Lady's bounty is for the picking and eating."

"So why?"

"I am not sure, a misunderstanding I think."

Rose stared at the stalls as they passed, and with more time she would have loved to investigate the many strange wares on display. A tall woman, wrapped in furs and draped in charms offered Pennyroyal, Mandrake and love potions. "Your voice, a pint of blood or your virginity." She was enfolded in a multitude of strange spices, some of which Rose recognised. Cinnamon and ginger flickered at her attention, but she had to be rushed away by Kye from a sweet cloud that made her dizzy.

"What was that?"

"I am not sure," Willow said. "An enchantment potion I think."

"Are you all right, Rose?" Lightning asked, handing Rose a cup of apple tea.

"I think so, but can we get out of this market, it's giving me a headache."

Lightning smiled and taking the thimble sized cup back, handed it to a five inch tall woman who winked at Rose with pin sized eyes.

"We are almost at the treeline."

He was right, they had cleared the market stalls and reached the scattering of low buildings that clustered at the roots of the massive trees. These buildings were little more than shacks though they all looked homely and none of them appeared abandoned or dirty. Rose saw that here there were huge mushrooms that were themselves homes. Many of the lizard-men squatted atop them and another of the tiny people glanced out of a door in the stalk of one particularly large mushroom, and seeing Willow Skin beckon, led out their family of ten. As they passed the low huts and toadstools their occupants flowed out and joined in a long line that began to grow in length as many new travellers arrived to swell their ranks.

"Is everyone here going where we are?"

"Yes, we are going to see the King and Queens," Moonstone said, and held out an apple to a lizard-man who plucked it from her hand with his tongue.

"Hang on," Eloo said, as they came up with her. "There's a bottleneck while the trees empty."

They had passed the lines of mushrooms and were now nearly at the feet of the trees. Rose studied the tree nearest her, to see that a staircase had been carved into the trunk and down this and rope ladders were descending a horde of strange creatures.

She looked higher to see that among the branches high above her head there were platforms and huts of tree houses, all emptying of their inhabitants.

"You mean people live up there?"

"Of course," Lea said as he appeared at her side. "Why not, after all, your people used to do it."

Rose might have replied to this, if she could think of a suitable response. So she turned her attention to the creatures coming down from the trees. She watched a man sized raven lead a large family of squirrels down the steps.

"Animals, too, are going?"

"Of course," Willow Skin said, surprised at this question. "They too have a voice at the court."

"What, you mean an actual voice?" Rose asked, as she remembered Kye talking to the wolf back at his tree house.

"Yes, they are represented by the animal nobles."

"Animal nobles?"

"You will see, but anyway that is not an ordinary raven," Lightning cut in. "That is a Corvion."

"A what?"

"A Ravennia," he tried again, looking at her as if she should know what he was talking about.

"Never heard of one," Rose said, staring at the giant bird that had stalked closer.

"A ravenman," Lea clarified.

As Lea said this, Rose realised that the bird's wing had a kind of hand on the end and that its claw like fingers were holding a bell, which it was ringing.

"You mean that that thing is a..."

Rose could not quite bring herself to say what was passing in her mind.

"He is as intelligent and civilised as you or me," Willow Skin said, smiling at Rose's shocked expression.

Rose looked back at the huge bird, noticing that its large, dark, beady eye was regarding her with a remarkable amount of intelligence and curiosity.

"Things just get weirder and weirder!"

"You haven't seen half of it yet!" Lightning chuckled, as they followed Kye past the tree stairs.

Once they made it through the trees that formed a ring around the base of the hill, they came upon a road. Not a foot trodden path, but a stone paved road, that circled the hill. Before them was a ring of stone arches or standing stones and capstones that towered twenty feet into the air and which cast long shadows.

"Do we go through there?" Rose asked, shivering, for she had heard of such stone circles and despite everything she had seen and heard Rose could not rid herself of the fear of such places.

"Eventually," Lea said. "After all, the rest of the city is in there."

"But not now," Willow Skin said, watching Kye consulting a tall girl dressed in the same browns and who had a similar appearance to Silver Skin, though she had no silver hair. Her hair was blonde.

"That isn't another member of your family, is it Lea?"

"Starshean? No," Lea said, with a grin. "No, she is from another pack, but she is a scout of the Silver Shield."

Kye saluted the girl and turning, pointed to the north and Lea nodded back.

"As I thought," Lea said. "We will be going past the city and to the lakeside thrones."

"Aren't the thrones in the city?"

"The King and Queens do have seats in the city, but they usually prefer to meet at the meeting points."

"Lightning, how often do these King and Queens meet?"

"They often hold court every month, but this is a Moot and means it is an unusual occasion."

They followed Kye as he led them round the stone circle, picking up other creatures on the way. Rose stopped and watched as a figure stepped out from one of the arches before her. This woman was either wearing a skimpy, if skin tight, green costume or, as Rose suspected, most of her skin was not skin, but glistening green scales.

"Lady Lamia," Lightning said, bowing to her. "I see the Moot has even drawn you from Hades. Is your mother here, too?"

As the woman watched Lightning bow, the amount of skin Rose could see expanded and shrank as the glittering scales slivered across her body. Whether the green scales were her flesh or living clothing Rose was not certain, but one thing was sure, she appeared practically naked save a belt around her handspan waist. Her expression was difficult to read, for the upper part of her face was concealed behind a mask of dark scales that once again might have been her skin or a piece of clothing. Her eyes were the deep green eyes of a snake and from her large mouth there flicked a long, forked tongue. When she opened her mouth unusually wide to speak, her voice was soft and hissing, like that of a snake.

"Lightning, a pleasure as always. No, my mother is not here, she is keeping guard of her charges, but she sent me as her representative."

"Would you wish to join our party?" Eloo asked, bouncing on the balls of her feet.

"Thank you, Princess Eloo, but I am waiting for my brother and then we shall go onto the Moot."

"No doubt we shall see you later."

"I look forward to it."

The rest of the party moved on, but as Rose passed by the snake woman, a long sinewy hand shot out and grasped Rose's wrist in an iron grip. Her long tongue flicked out and her large, green slitted eyes stared unblinkingly into Rose's.

"A Spark," hissed the woman.

"Lady Lamia, this is Rose, a new friend of ours. She is coming with us to the Moot," Lightning said, and gently took Rose's arm and steered her away.

The snake woman gave Rose a last flick of her tongue and letting go of Rose's wrist turned away and into the shadows of the arch.

"Who was that?" Rose asked, massaging her wrist.

"That is Lady Lamia," Lea said, waving at Lor who was several yards further along the stone ring.

"Who is her mother... Medusa?"

"No, Medusa is her aunt," Lightning said, deadpan. "Her mother is Campe."

"Who?"

"Ask me again later and I'll explain."

"And why did she call me a Spark and what is one of those?"

"Now is neither the time nor the place, Rose," Lightning said, watching Silver beckon them.

"Okay, but you had better tell me later or I am going to be very annoyed."

Rose nodded and with the rest of the party, moved to join Lor and Silver Skin, who were standing further along the circle.

"Kye, you will be pleased to hear that the nest of goblins has been cleared," Silver said, as they came up to them.

"Good," Kye grunted, but he didn't look happy. "Do we know how many were killed?"

"I have not heard numbers."

Kye grunted, and turning away from Silver led them along the stone path.

"Lea, why isn't Kye pleased to hear this news?"

"Who knows, I, too, find my older brother as unreadable as you do. But if I were to guess, I would say Kye is not convinced we have heard the last of those orcs."

"Haven't we?"

Lea shrugged. "You tell me."

"Well, I would like to know how much further to wherever we are going?"

"A few more yards and we will be at the East gate. Look, just there."

Rose followed his pointing finger, to see a few yards to the left a similar set of doors to those they had exited the day before. Even as Rose saw them, a flash of movement at the corner of her eye made her turn to see emerging from one of the arches of the stone ring a huge giant of a man that surprised her. She was not surprised by this man's size, no, what surprised her was the bull's head atop his shoulders.

"Then they do exist," Rose murmured, watching the Minotaur stride towards the doors, his horns grazing the lintel as he pulled them open. He held one side of the doors open, to allow a pair of trolls to pass before him and then he disappeared into the darkness beyond.

"Rose, when you've picked your jaw off the floor, perhaps you might like to go through the gate," Lightning said, his voice full of amusement.

Rose snorted and followed him through the massive door to the white tunnel beyond. It resembled the one they had used to enter the city, with the one exception that there were no gates at the end, just a thick mist hanging like a veil before them, but which gave no resistance as they pushed through it to emerge in bright sunlight on the other side.

THE SYLVAN THRONE

"Gods and Goddesses may take on mortal form and yet still be powers
apart. Still, their bodies can bleed and die."
Artemis to the Red Wizard, the Wereding Chronicles.

hen Rose stopped blinking she saw before her a wide
open space like a three tiered amphitheatre, which
opened towards the lake in a three sided crescent. Below,
in the centre of the theatre, were four thrones carved from giant tree
stumps. All the tiers of the raised levels were filled with hundreds of
the strange members of the nations. Among the seated hundreds, she
recognised dwarfs, gnomes, minotaurs, and different kinds of troll,
some with black skin like obsidian, others with jagged protrusions
like stalagmites. There was a group of the tall, statuesque amazon
women and towering over all were the giants.

Rose felt a shadow pass over her and looking up saw that in the
air above them and the meeting place there were dozens of birds,
or were they other creatures? Rose watched as one of them came to
hover before them, level with where they stood. It was not strictly
speaking a bird, but it was not quite a woman either. It had a pair
of fiery red wings, but it also had a large pair of breasts and its head
was not that of a bird, but a beautiful woman. Her coppery red skin
glowed in the sunlight.

"Mistress Takana," Lightning cried out, and lifted his hand in
salute.

The beautiful creature lifted her leg and Rose saw that it was more
like a human hand than a bird's foot, though it had long talons. On
one of these finger-toes there flashed a ring, and from it there shot
a beam of light that connected her ring to Lightning's, and for a
moment Lightning's eyes rolled back in his head.

"Lightning, are you all right?"

"He's fine, Rose," Eloo said, coaxing her away. "He and Takana are
just communicating, that's all."

"Communicating how?"

"Through the rings," Lightning said, as the woman broke the link and turning, stooped into the partial circle to land beside the throne that stood alone, facing the other three.

"Who, or what, was that?"

"Takana," Eloo explained. "One of the harpies, and the mistress of the fire school."

"She's a harpy?"

"One of them, yes."

"She's not what I imagined."

"We are and are not, the creatures of your myths," Kye said.

"I guess so," Rose said, not quite sure she understood him. "Those must be the thrones, right?"

"Those are the Sylvan Thrones," Kye grunted.

"So, where are the King and Queens?"

"They will be here shortly," Eloo said, searching the steps as though looking for someone.

Rose, too, stared at the floor of the semicircle and saw a narrow path that separated the horns of the circle from the waters of the dark lake and which led off to the left and right and into the many willows that framed the water.

"There they are." Eloo sighed with relief as she found what she was seeking.

Rose followed Eloo's pointing wand, to see that from the willows on the southern path there were emerging a twin row of figures that padded out into the semi-circle, where they formed an arch of honour with long swords for a figure slowly, almost reluctantly trotting from the willows behind them.

At first Rose did not see this and she only noticed later, for now she only had eyes for the honour guard. For although she had heard Lightning's description of the Furies, a description is never quite the same thing as seeing with your own eyes. So she stared at these magnificent creatures standing below her. Her imagination had been close and yet not close enough.

They were Amazons, beautiful, with long hair knotted and braided in strange designs, their beautiful curves emphasised rather than concealed by their close fitting leather armour. Their lower bodies were those of huge black panthers or the tawny flanks of Lionesses.

Rose could have stared for hours at these beautiful, if terrible cat Centaurs, if Eloo's voice had not drawn her attention to the rider who came behind and between this guard.

"Here she comes!"

Rose tore her gaze away from the head Fury, who stood closest to the nearest throne (she was a panther with raven black hair), and fixed her eyes on the woman who was slowly and proudly riding up the arch, to dismount and take the throne. Once again Rose did not immediately notice the rider because she was absorbed by the woman's mount, a horse of such brilliant white that it dazzled the eye, and from this beautiful horse's forehead protruded a long spiralling horn that looked like a tiny lance.

"A unicorn!" Rose breathed.

"Yes, Artemis can still ride them. I have lost that pleasure, right, Kye?" Eloo said, grinning cheekily at her lover.

"Shush, Eloo, you're spoiling the ritual," Lightning chided her.

Rose now turned her attention to the rider, who had dismounted the unicorn. She was taller than Eloo and was dressed in dark brown leathers and carried a horse bow, but from here she reminded her of someone. She flicked her gaze from Artemis to Eloo and back and could not shake the idea that they were the same. Like Great Mother, she had a long braid of silver hair that glittered in the light, and it and her brown cape were blown about by a wind that seemed to constantly swirl around her, though Rose could feel no wind on her face. It was as though she had her own personal breeze, an idea strengthened by the fact that the Furies' hair and capes were not moving, though they stood only a few feet from the figure.

"So, that is one of the Queens, is it?"

"Yes, though as Selene's daughter she is co-ruler. That is Artemis, the embodiment of the Maiden."

"Look, here comes Hecate," Lea said, pointing.

Rose watched as from the same point a throne was carried by four huge, giant like figures. Rose blinked as she saw the figure in the seat. It was a wizened thing that might be male or female, so old and wrinkled was it that it was impossible to tell. Its long white hair was a stark contrast to the dark brown leather like skin.

"Who is that?"

"Hecate, the Queen of crones. Look, she has brought the Graeae with her."

Rose followed Lea's pointing finger, to see that following the carrying chair were three tall figures. They appeared to be tall, very old women, dressed in grey robes and carrying long, gnarled staffs.

"Are they witches?"

"The Graeae are three sisters," Eloo said in a hiss. "They are the oldest and most powerful of their kind, and they should be cast out into the outer darkness."

"Why, are they evil?"

"Eloo believes so," Lightning said.

"Well, they are," Eloo said angrily. "If they weren't Hecate's advisors they would have been killed long ago."

"Eloo, watch your tongue," Kye warned.

"No, I won't."

"Eloo, look, I think Selene is on her way," Lor said, pointing to the waterside.

Rose saw the unicorn leave its rider's side and trot to the lake where it dropped its head to dip its horn into the lake and was stirring the water with it. As Rose watched, ripples were sent flickering out into the lake. As if in answer to this stirring, the lake birthed a great spout of water. Rose watched and blinked as a plume of water shot high into the air and something huge darted from the water spout. Rose watched with shocked awe as a creature similar to the Fire Drake swooped out of the water spout and dropped down to land before the central throne.

"What is that?"

"A Water Wyrm," Lightning said.

"It is Moon Flower, Selene's steed."

Rose stared down at the huge beast that dripped water from its dark scales. The Water Dragon resembled a huge otter like creature, complete with long whiskers, though apart from a lion like mane, its body was covered with scales, not fur. It folded a pair of huge, green, feathered wings close into its blue-black scales, its large green eyes glaring at everything around it.

"Will it attack?"

"What, Moon Flower?" Eloo asked, a touch of amazement in her voice. "No, not unless we threaten her mistress."

"Mistress?"

"Selene."

Rose became aware of a rider mounted on the dragon's back. As she watched, this tall, silver haired woman leapt down from its back. She stood for a moment against the dark side of the dragon, and Rose noticed a faint silvery glow flickering around her. She was reminded of the silvery woman she had dreamed of only a few nights ago.

"Eloo, are you related to these women?" Rose asked, staring at the woman sitting in the middle throne and the huge dragon padding round the back to curl around it, like a snake or dog, its head lying before its mistress' feet.

"Of course I am," Eloo said with surprise. "Selene is my mother, Artemis is my sister and Hecate is my grandmother. I thought you knew that?"

"You forget how little Rose knows about our people," Silver said gently.

"Sister," Rose whispered, suddenly aware that her sister was missing. At that moment, she would have given up all these amazing experiences to see Robin's face. Rose felt very lonely and was glad for Lightning's distraction.

"The Queens are here, so all we need is the King," Lightning said, looking towards the lake.

"Lightning, who is the King, and is he Eloo's father?" Rose asked in a soft whisper.

However, Rose had not estimated just how good Eloo's hearing was, for with a giggle she answered for him.

"Rose, my Father is Hunter, and here he comes."

As Eloo said this, from the opposite side to which the two Queens had appeared came an honour guard of centaurs of every colour imaginable. Their long swords gleamed only slightly more than their glossy flanks.

"The Silver Shield do scrub up well, don't they?"

"Shush, he comes," Kye said, almost reverently.

Rose watched as the centaurs lifted their swords so they formed a very high arch, though the creature advancing up the arch still brushed the blades with his horns. At first Rose thought the King was riding a huge stag, then that he was a huge stag, but when he stepped beyond the centaurs Rose saw she was wrong on both counts. The huge figure that strode to the single throne was a giant of a man. He must have been seven feet tall, but his height was made even more imposing by the set of stag antlers sprouting from his fiery haired head.

174

"That's your father?"

"That is the Hunter," Eloo said, a huge smile splitting her face. "And he is father to us all."

Rose watched as this giant moved with animal grace to the huge carved throne that faced the three queens. As he sat, Rose noticed he wore a horn on a baldric and a knife was strapped to his left leg, but apart from this he appeared quite naked. A jet black giant who had come behind him stood between the thrones and unfurled a standard of an antlered dragon and announced in a voice like thunder, "All behold defender of the faith, lord protector, and warden of the west and hand of the Horned God, Hunter Moriganhand."

Following this grandiose announcement, the huge Hunter raised the horn to his lips and gave a mighty blast that seemed to fill the world with its loud, deep note.

"That means the Moot has begun," Kye said, and without another word he and Eloo disappeared among the crowds of the nations.

"Where are they going?"

"Both Kye and Eloo would speak to the court," Lightning said, sinking down on the edge of the first step, his pipe smoking as he drew on it.

"Should we go with them?"

"Not unless we are summoned," Lea said, sitting beside Lightning.

Rose, feeling that she stood out, sank down beside Lightning, but she could not tear her eyes away from what was happening below. The huge stag-man let the horn lie on his knees, and drawing the hunting knife from its sheath cast it at his feet.

"That is a symbol that the Hunter lays down his power and submits to the people."

Rose was about to ask what would happen next, when the amphitheatre was filled with a voice like thunder. "Peoples of the nations, you have been summoned by the will of the Lady Selene. Do you love her?"

Rose realised this was the Hunter's voice. A voice answered by a roar of shouting in response. "We love our Queens and King," was the thunderous reply.

"Then I ask the Lady Selene to tell us why she has called us to Moot."

WORDS OF THE HORNED QUEEN

"Silver haired Lady, you who bear the horns of the crescent moon, please speak to us and enrich us with your wise words."
A prayer to the Horned Lady, from the Book of the Wolf.

Selene rose, the light gleaming off a pair of small horns projecting from her temples.

"So that's why they call her the Horned Lady?"

"Shush," Silver said, from behind Rose.

When Selene spoke, her voice filled the tiered meeting place like the Hunter's, but unlike the Hunter's thunderous voice Selene's voice was a soft whisper that made Rose think of wind shivering through leaves, or waves lapping at a shore.

"Thank you, my Lord, thank you, my people. I love you with all my heart. I have summoned you here because I have received troubling messages from the Goddess."

"It seems that Selene has had the same sending you did, Rose," Lightning whispered in her ear.

"I and the other Queens have all sensed a change, a movement of the elements that portent some terrible event threatening us all."

At this, a murmur of concern rumbled its way through the massed beings. At the edge of the thrones' clearing, a tall man stood. Rose would have thought he was a normal man, but for the fact that instead of hair, a large feathery crest stood high from his skull.

"Does the Silver Lady say what this threat is?"

"No, Knight Gold Fan, she does not. Only that her power may be reduced and so she may not be able to help us."

"Kye always says that gods help those who help themselves," Lea muttered.

"What of the Silver Claws, do they know nothing?" This question was put by Lamia, who hissed it from the edge of the tiers.

There was a bustling at the edge of the circle and what Rose had thought were several large boulders transformed into large lizard men. The largest of these had turned a jet black, but as it stepped forwards and held out its hands, its long claw like fingernails glittered silver in the sunlight.

"My King," said this lizard man, or was it a woman with that high voice? "I have been searching for threats and I believe I have found it."

"Then speak, Alal Silverhand," boomed the Hunter. "Tell us what you have perceived."

"Not I, my lord, but one of my Silver Claws has discovered this terrible truth."

"Bring him forth, so that we may hear the truth from his lips."

At this, Silverhand turned to its left and beckoned a steadily brightening red lizard forwards.

"Skinspeaker, isn't it?" Silver Skin said in surprise.

The bright red lizard kept its eyes low and spoke in a whisper that only the silver handed lizard lord heard, but she spoke for him.

"You must forgive Skinspeaker, my lord, he is very shy," Silverhand explained.

"Will he speak through you?"

"If you would be so good, my lord."

"Proceed."

"I and my brothers were sent to the great tomb to check on rumours that the Darkling kin were flourishing. We hoped to find nothing but a few goblins, but unfortunately, we found in one of the under halls hundreds of goblins and worse, numberless orcs…"

The Silverhand's words were drowned out by a roar of anger and the gathered nation broke into countless conversations, though Rose could make out some crying that it wasn't possible.

"Silence!" roared the Hunter. "Silverhand, is this Skinspeaker sure of what he saw?"

Silverhand did not hesitate, though Skinspeaker at her side shrank back and disappeared, becoming the dark brown of the earth around him.

"My lord, Skinspeaker is one of my best Talons. He has served the Silver Claws for twenty years and has always served me well. I will give my word that his word is good. Besides this, his brothers confirm what he says."

"And where are his brothers?" the feathered man asked.

"One of them died in the ruins, the other is still healing from a poisoned arrow. In short, my lords, these Silver Claws risked much to bring us this dreadful, though true news."

"We understand, Silverhand, we shall not forget their sacrifice."

"You are gracious, my lord," Silverhand said, bowing her head and retreating to join the rest of the lizard men, who greeted her return with the flicking of tongues and bright flashes of colour.

"So now we know," Hunter boomed, turning his attention to the Queens. "The maggots have been breeding. Very well, a force must be sent into the rats nest to wipe them out."

"My lord, I would speak, if I may." It was Kye's voice and it croaked from behind Selene's throne.

"Who would speak? Reveal yourself," boomed the Hunter.

Kye stepped forth, his hands held empty before him. He came unarmed to the King. A thing that was well, for Rose saw the Centaurs at Hunter's side draw their bows.

"Ah, it is one of the Silverbrow children, is it not?"

Kye came closer to the Elven King and at a respectful distance went down on one knee.

"Kye, my lord," Kye whispered.

Rose wondered how she was able to hear Kye, for he was still using his hoarse whisper, but she could hear him as clearly as if he was standing beside her.

"Well, what would you say to us?"

"My lord, even if the army of the dark was a thousand times greater than Skinspeaker believes it to be, it would not be a threat to the Silver Lady, and yet she believes her power will be diminished."

"Your point?"

"That there is something about these events not yet revealed. My lord, all my senses tell me that the orcs are only the hand of some darker power."

Kye's words made the Hunter think, but not for long.

"Do you have any proof of this?"

"No, my lord, no proof, except my heart."

"Then I am afraid that is not enough. I must deal with the threats I can see before I deal with greater threats."

Kye bowed and rising, turned to go, when the horned Selene stopped him.

"Kye, if you feel you should pursue this line of thought, do so."

"As you wish, my Queen," whispered the tall werewolf.

"In the meantime, we must prepare for war," Hunter shouted. "Where is my Lord of War?"

There was a commotion at the edge of the circle and a large group of armed Centaurs parted to reveal a creature like and unlike them.

"What in heaven and earth is that?"

"His name is Manticore," Lightning chuckled into her ear. "And he is a Drakaina and Lamia's brother."

Manticore was like a Centaur, in that his lower body was not human, but there the resemblance ended, for the Manticore's lower body was that of a dragon, complete with green scales, huge batwings, and a long serpentine tail that ended in a large barbed point. His upper body was human, well, just, for the more Rose stared at him the more she was reminded of a Lion. His skin was a dark brown and his long mane of hair tawny, his huge eyes yellow and his pupils vertical slits. When he spoke, long canines flashed in the light. He was wearing a large breastplate emblazoned with a winged lion and the tower shield that he wore like a buckler was also painted with this design. This monster stood well over six feet tall and if the bulging muscles weren't proof enough of his great strength, the war hammer he was carrying must have had a haft as long as her arm.

"Ah, Manticore, what do you advise, my general?" Hunter asked as Manticore padded before him.

For a long time the man-dragon did not answer, but simply padded back and forth. After a long pause he spoke in a deep growling voice that sounded as if it had come from the bowels of a wild beast. "Until I have other reports I cannot be sure, my lord, but based on the current assessment I would withdraw all our people still living between the ruins and the wall and rebuild the old redoubt."

"That sounds good," Hunter said, turning his knife over in his huge hands. "But what of the lands to the east and west of the burnt land?"

"There is a small kingdom to the east, but it comes under the protection of the human domain," broke in one of the tall centaurs at the King's side.

"Then that is a human concern."

"I think it might be best to order a travel ban south of the King's," growled Manticore.

"Agreed, no one should pass the Twin gates," Hunter agreed.

"I am afraid this will cause problems," said a new voice, soft but powerful, like a sheathed sword.

Both Hunter and Manticore turned towards the voice that came from behind the throne.

"Takana," Hunter said, his large mouth curling at the edges. "What is your problem?"

"You would forbid any of our people, except your spies and scouts, from leaving our lands and travelling south?"

"Yes, why, do you have a problem with this?"

"Not myself, but I think several of your subjects may have a problem with it."

This tore an animalistic snarl from Manticore. "They will have to obey."

"And they probably would, normally, but they have given an oath to go beyond these lands."

"Please, Takana, stop dancing round the point," Hunter rumbled. "What are you driving at and who are you speaking for?"

"He can speak for himself," the Harpy said, lifting one of her wings and pointing with a finger tipped wing towards where Kye and Eloo sat at Selene's feet. "Kye, I believe you have given your word to a certain lady."

"How does she know about that?"

"Through the rings," Lightning said. "The mind link allows her to see all that I have experienced in the last few days. She must have perceived this."

Rose wanted to ask Lightning more about this link, but her attention was diverted by Kye's actions. The black haired werewolf stood and came to stand near to Manticore, but his eyes were on Hunter.

"I think my lord is aware of the young lady I and your daughter found in the birches several days ago."

"Yes, your mother has kept me informed of your actions, what of it?"

"Then perhaps Great Mother has mentioned that Rose had a vision showing her sister becoming a member of the Crimson Circle?"

"I don't recall it."

"That is because I did not know it," said Great Mother, appearing at Takana's side. "How did she have this vision?"

"She used the Wand of Wisdom," Kye said, meeting his mother's eyes.

"So the rumours are true!" Rose heard a voice say from below her. She looked down to see the mutterer was a tiny troll.

"How does this have bearing on the ban?"

"It has bearing, my lord, because I promised to do everything within my power to remove this child from the dark brotherhood."

"That was foolish," Manticore growled.

"Foolish, perhaps," Selene said from her throne, "but oft the foolish do wise acts and the wise may say and do foolish things. No one can see what their actions will lead to, not the great Hunter and wise Manticore."

Hunter bowed his antlered head in his Queen's direction. "As always, my lady, your wisdom drops like gentle rain."

"Foolish or not," growled Manticore, "it means Kye will leave our ranks to go on a pointless mission. Can we throw away even one bow and blade?"

"Not just one blade," Silver said, and rose to her feet. "I, too, have pledged myself to this task."

"And I," Lightning shouted, rising to join Silver.

"And I." Lea rose.

"And I too," Lor said, appearing at his brother's side.

Rose's eyes blurred as she realised that each of her companions was ready to help her rescue Robin. However, it appeared Manticore was not pleased by this.

"Has the entire Silverbrow family lost their minds?"

"Not all," Great Mother said from Takana's side. "Still, Lord Manticore, if my children have given their word, there is nothing you or I can do to stop them."

"Has any other pledged themselves to this pointless task?"

"I," Eloo said, and stepped up beside her lover, her green eyes glowing like a cat's in the dimming light. "And by my word no one, not even you, Manticore, will stop us."

Manticore snarled and might have said something if the Hunter had not spoken.

"Where is this Rose?"

"Here," Rose heard herself say, rising to her feet, not believing what she was doing, but doing it nonetheless.

"Come here, child," Hunter said glancing up at her. "I would like to meet the one who can bind the Black Bow to a quest."

THE QUEST OF THE ROBIN

"To see a Robin is easy in winter, but in summer, all you can find is his voice."
Kye, from the Wereding Chronicles by the Red Wizard.

R ose stared down at the stag like giant that was the Hunter, and quailed. He had asked her to come to him, but she couldn't bring herself to do so.

"Come, child," he commanded and his words felt like chains, binding her to his will and pulling her towards him. "I won't bite."

"Come, Rose," Lightning whispered to her, as he gently, but firmly took her arm and guided her towards a ramp that descended to the next level. "He won't hurt you, but the Lord of the hunt is not known for his patience. Best not to keep him waiting."

"Lightning," Rose whispered as she was led down a broad ramp to the next level of the wide tiers. "I'm afraid."

"Of Hunter?"

"Yes."

"Don't be, he looks intimidating, but he won't hurt you."

"Are you sure of that?"

"Well, actually, now you come to mention it, no. But I promise you this, I won't let him."

Rose glanced from Lightning's tall, wiry frame to the huge giant that was Hunter. There should be no way Lightning would be able to defend her from Hunter, but somehow Rose believed Lightning meant it.

"You promise?"

"I promise. Cross my heart and hope to die."

That made Rose turn her gaze from the hordes of strange beings that were parting for them to his face, and in particular his green eyes.

"Don't say that. I don't want you to die."

From behind them Silver's voice broke into this tender moment. "Rose, watch out, you're on the edge of a ramp."

Rose looked down to see that she was right, and stepping onto the ramp, she descended to the floor of the amphitheatre and saw before her the thrones. Eloo beckoned to her, smiling as if she was enjoying every moment of this.

"Come, child, let me see you."

Rose was drawn, almost against her will, by Hunter's soft, powerful voice. She was standing on the edge of the huge semi-circle, and the next moment she was standing before the throne and the giant filling it. Rose had been presented to the king at court by her father when only five and she felt now as she had done then, shy and afraid, so she kept her eyes lowered so as not to meet Hunter's eyes and she bowed low.

"Look up, my child, I won't turn you to stone," rumbled the giant elf king.

Rose slowly and reluctantly raised her eyes to meet his. Hunter's eyes were those of a hawk. Rose could think of no other words to describe them. They were yellow, no, golden, and their pupils were like the mythical black holes her tutors used to tell her about and which were supposed to suck everything into themselves. These eyes sucked at her, drawing her in as though they wanted to swallow her whole. Rose felt herself falling into them and forgetting any courtesy, jerked her gaze away and down to her boots. Her cheeks flushed with embarrassment. An embarrassment that only made Hunter explode with laughter that rocked his whole body.

"Forgive me, child, I did not realise I was testing you."

"Hunter, that's not fair," Takana chided him. "The child is not used to your eyes, and you should not probe her that way."

"Perhaps, my fire lady, perhaps. Still, I learned one thing."

"And what was that?"

"That her heart is pure and a lovely thing too. She has captured Lightning's heart it seems and now I think I understand how."

"Does that mean we can go?" Lea asked.

"It means I will consider it," Hunter said, glaring at the young werewolf.

"My lord, I would counsel you against sending the Silverbrow twins," Manticore growled. "They have only just taken their place in the ranks."

"Does that mean that we don't have a right to join Kye?" Lea asked, clearly not happy with the chance that he would be left behind.

"It means, pup," Manticore snarled, "that you are pledged to serve the Elven people. It means you are under orders from your officer."

"Who happens to be Kye," Silver Skin said gently.

"Who is under the command of his superior," Manticore shot back.

"That happens to be my honour," growled a voice from opposite the throne.

Rose had heard this voice before. It bubbled up out of the earth like a geyser and hung in the air like a mist. It was Flash speaking.

Rose glanced over her shoulder to see the giant glaring at Kye's back with yellow eyes.

"And you are under my command, Flash," Manticore growled.

"Peace, Manticore," Hunter said, his gaze going past Kye to Flash. "Flash, what are your wishes in this matter?"

Flash did not at once respond, his yellow eyes staring beyond his king, and following his gaze Rose realised he was looking to Great Mother for guidance. Rose saw no signal pass between the giant werewolves, but perhaps there was none.

"I would say Kye is allowed to command his own soldiers as he sees fit. However, neither he nor I are beyond the will of the people and your Highness's pleasure."

"Kye?"

Kye, too, sought Great Mother's gaze and judgement, but if she gave any, Rose could not see it.

"I, too, submit to the King's wisdom," Kye whispered, though more reluctantly.

"At last wisdom prevails," Manticore purred.

"That remains to be seen," Takana's voice cut in.

"Enough, Takana, I will think on this matter and decide before sunrise," Hunter growled. "Is there any other business?"

"There were many matters of state, my lord," the lead centaur said. "However, I believe protocol maintains that they must wait until matters of war are settled."

"Very well, the court is dismissed," Hunter boomed.

As if by magic, the amphitheatre cleared and apart from the King, the Queens and their guards and councillor, Rose and her companions were alone in the huge semi-circle.

"Come on, Rose, let's get out of here," Lightning whispered, as they watched Hunter surrounded by Manticore and the rest of his Centaurs. "They will be talking about war and won't want us."

"What will he decide?"

"Who can say?"

Rose wanted to go to him and beg him to let them go, but she was not sure if she could bring herself to face those eyes again.

"He will make up his own mind, Rose," Lightning said, sensing her thoughts. "There is nothing you or I can say to change it. Come, let us prepare for the journey."

"A journey that will never happen."

They were turning to go when Selene's voice came to them on the wind. "Rose, I would speak with you."

DRAGON'S BREATH

"Whether dragons breathe fire or ice they still bring death."
The Druids' Handbook.

Rose turned to find the eyes of the Elven Queen on her. As with Hunter, she felt drawn to the silver haired woman who watched her approach with eyes like silver coins. Rose came to stand only a few feet from the tall woman's throne. She was very aware of the dragon just to her right.

As she approached, the huge beast raised its head slightly to turn a green eye on Rose. Rose trembled as she felt its presence, cold but burning with an intensity Rose had not felt before. But after a moment's inspection, the dragon returned its head to the resting place of its paws.

Rose's attention was drawn from the dragon back to the Elven Queen, as her soft whisper rustled in her ear. "Greetings, Rose, well met, my daughter."

Rose opened her mouth to say Selene was not her mother, but remembering Lightning had said Hunter was a father to them all, she hesitated.

Selene watched her with those silver eyes. "I heard you have a question for me, young one?"

"A question," Rose whispered, feeling the weight of those eyes upon her.

"Your hand," Lightning whispered from behind her.

"Oh, yes my hand," Rose said, raising her hand before her, showing the dark scales on its back.

"You will have to turn your hand over, my dear, I cannot see it from here," said the Queen softly and with gentleness.

Rose slowly, almost reluctantly, turned her hand so the back was facing Selene. As her silver glowing eyes fell on it, a faint sigh hissed from between her lips.

"What is it?"

"It appears, child, that you are a Spark."

Rose's patience broke and for a moment she forgot she was in the presence of a Queen. "Will someone around here tell me what the hell this Spark means? Everyone keeps saying I'm a Spark as if I should know what it means, and I don't. So will someone tell me, am I cursed or what?"

"Calm yourself, child," Selene said.

"No, I won't, I want some answers," Rose said, her voice rising.

As Rose's voice rose in anger the dragon's head lifted to face her. Its huge jaws swung open to release a gust of cold air that felt like it had come from the legendary wastes of the north. As it did, a hiss came from the dragon like the steaming of a hundred kettles. Rose suddenly felt the giant presence of the dragon and was afraid and angry at the same time. The next instant, her voice was ringing out across the semi-circle and suddenly and beyond her comprehension she was sheathed in a halo of dancing blue flames that drove back the chill of the dragon's breath.

Rose looked through the sheen of flames and felt herself falling. When she came to it was to find herself staring up into a beautiful, if strange face. The face gazed back at her with green cat eyes and its cat like ears twitched. Rose thought for a moment that it was Eloo, but it was not the right shape. Slowly, she realised it was the face of the head Fury.

"She is coming round," the face said in a deep gravelly voice.

"Thank you, Lara, you can let her up now."

Rose became aware that she could not move because she was being pinned to the ground by the Fury's body.

"Please, get off," Rose groaned, for she was finding it difficult to breathe under the Fury's weight.

"Only if you will not use your magic against the Queen," growled the cat woman, her lips peeling back to reveal long canines.

"I won't."

"Promise."

"Get off her, Lara," Lightning said harshly. "She did not even know she was doing it. Your mistress is in no danger."

"Promise."

"I promise," Rose breathed.

As soon as she breathed these words the weight was gone, and so was the face.

Lightning pulled her to her feet and dusted her down. "Are you all right?"

"I think so," Rose whispered.

In truth, she did not feel well. She felt as though she had run all day. The wind had been knocked out of her and she felt bruised. She gingerly touched her ribs.

"Do you need healing?"

"I don't think so, just a good rest. What happened?"

"You conjured a fireskin," the Fury growled from in front of Selene, using her body as a physical shield against Rose.

"Behold the Red Wizard," cried Takana's mocking voice.

"Not again," Rose moaned, and lifting her arm with difficulty she stared at the back of her hand, groaning as she saw the red scales had spread to cover not just the first set of knuckles, but across the back of her hand almost to the wrist, and long ribbon like tendrils had begun to snake along her fingers and past the wrist.

"What is this?"

"The side effects of your nature," Selene said from behind the Fury. "Lara, please, get out of the way. Sparks often do not have control of their powers at first."

"My lady, she is a threat," growled the Fury.

"Lara, please, I wish to speak to her face to face and lovely as your back is, I would rather look at Rose's face at the moment."

Reluctantly, the Fury slid sideways, so that Rose was once again facing Selene.

"Rose, you are a Spark, the descendant of a dragon."

"What?" Rose asked, not believing what she was hearing. It couldn't be true, she couldn't be hearing what she thought she was hearing. "No, that can't be true."

"Rose, the scales on the back of your hand prove that somewhere in your family's past, one of your relatives has mated with a dragon," Selene said, her eyes still kind despite their silvery glow.

"But my father wasn't and my mother, they were normal."

"The individual could have been hundreds of years ago. Sparks can skip generations. Is this not so, Lightning?"

"So I am taught, my Queen," Lightning said, offering Rose a flask.

Rose ignored the proffered bottle and stared at her transformed hand. This was proof that she had dragon's venom in her veins.

"That would explain the unknown magic use," Eloo said from Rose's other side.

"It would, my daughter, as usual your razor mind cuts to the point."

Rose was still trying to get over what she had just been told, but she could not resist asking what they were talking about.

"When the magic awakens in a Spark, it can surge out of control of the vessel. When it does this it has strange effects on the vessel," Selene explained.

"So, when I cast magic unwillingly, it changes me?"

"Yes, that appears to be the case," Lightning agreed.

"But why is this happening?"

"The magic inside you has acted to protect you from perceived threats, like when you and the magic thought Moonflower was going to attack you."

"Is there a way to stop this or turn it back?"

"I don't know of one," Eloo said, her gaze going from Lightning to Selene. "Do you, Mother?"

"Then what will happen to me? What will I become?"

"The scales will continue to spread until you are covered by them," Selene said, her voice full of compassion.

Rose saw in her mind's eye the image of Lamia, except the face under the mask of scales was her own.

Selene, seeing the tears welling up in her eyes, gave Rose hope. "I said there was no way to change you, but there may be a way to stop its spread."

"How?"

"The magic inside you is having this effect because it is building up with no way of escape until it breaks forth to protect you, and that is when its access changes you. If the magic was released regularly it would not build up in your skin and have this side effect."

"Does that mean I will have to learn magic?"

"I am afraid so," Lightning said. "I know you don't trust magic, Rose, but if you don't use your magic regularly it could build up to dangerous levels."

"Dangerous?"

"If magic is not allowed to have its way, it can build up and could have who knows what effect on you."

She glanced from Lightning to Selene, asking herself if what they were telling her was the truth. She couldn't quite bring herself to believe it, and yet, why would they lie to her? She knew she trusted Lightning, but she had never met Selene. Could she trust her? She met the Elven Queen's silver eyes and saw her thought mirrored there. The Elven Queen could read her thoughts.

"I have no reason to lie, Rose. I wish to help you."

The Fury, Lara, growled at the idea that her mistress might have lied.

"I am sorry," Rose said, dropping her eyes. "But I have not met you before. I ask myself, why I should trust you and—"

"And you say to yourself, I do not know this Selene," Selene said gently. "You have no reason to apologise, Rose. Trust must be earned, it is a gift if given without reason."

Rose blushed and stared at her hand. She clenched it into a fist and determined that she would not cry and would meet her fate with as much courage as she could muster. After all, that was how she thought her father would deal with such a situation. Thinking about her father stirred up a cloud of grief.

"What do I have to do?"

"Brave girl," Lightning said, slapping her on the back.

Rose forced a smile. Lightning's enthusiasm was helpful, but she still felt afraid.

"It all depends on how powerful the magic is inside you," Takana's voice said in her ear.

Rose jumped, and turning, found the tall bird woman standing behind her. Her dark green eyes met her own. As Rose stared into those eyes she felt as if she was looking into the woman's soul and it was a deep, dark and murky pit of mysteries.

"What did you say?"

"I said that what you will need to do to control the power depends on the level of power inside you."

"And how do we find that out?"

"Through experimentation," Takana explained. "Only you can find out what levels the power is and what it will take to ease the pressure."

"Okay, I have to find out myself, but how do I do that?"

"By learning and practising magic. The more magic you cast, the less it will build up in your body."

"And that will stop the scales from spreading?"

Takana's eyes darkened, as if a veil dropped across them. "Rose, I cannot promise you that. Nothing is certain when it comes to magic, but yes, under normal circumstances the scales should not grow more."

"But if I cast magic it might not happen?"

"That is what my researches have led me to believe, yes."

"When and how do I begin?"

"Lightning can begin to teach you on your journey," Selene said, from where she had closed her eyes, her attention leaving them. "If I know my Lightning, he has already given a few of our secrets away."

"Only the fire lighting spell!" Lightning said defensively.

This made Takana laugh loudly. "Oh, Lightning, you are a card and no mistake. Come, we appear to be tiring our queen. Let us go and prepare for your journey."

"Will there be a journey?"

Takana glanced to where Hunter was consulting with Manticore over a map drawn of silver and black lines that hovered in mid-air in front of them, though there appeared to be no paper on which it was drawn.

"Who can tell with Hunter? But always live in hope and you will be rewarded. Now come, I am hungry."

Rose watched Hunter draw a long finger along a silver line. The map rippled, as though he were causing a ripple in water. "How are they doing that?"

"What? The map?" Takana asked. "It is a simple, if helpful, projection of light."

"A what?"

"An illusion spell," Lightning clarified, leading Rose back across the open area to where the ramp led up to now empty terraces.

"When will Hunter let us know what he has decided?"

"The King will tell us when he wishes," Lightning said, preceding Rose up the ramp. "No one makes his mind up for him. However, he did say he would decide by sunrise."

"Will he let us go?"

"I don't know, Rose. Eloo might know better than I, but I expect that not even his daughter can tell which way he will jump."

"You are quite right there, L. Father will make up his own mind and what it is I wouldn't guess. But like Takana says, Rose, hope and we will see what we shall see."

"Don't worry, Rose," Lightning whispered in her ear. "Even if Hunter decides against you, I will take you south. If your sister is in trouble I will help you and her."

Rose, heartened by Lightning's words, turned to gaze out over the arena and the lake. From the top of the terraces she could see far out over the lake and to the south. Somewhere out there Robin was in trouble and Rose swore to herself she would help her.

Under her breath she spoke such an oath. "We're coming, Robin, hang in there. I promise we're coming, just hang on. I'm coming to save you – I swear that on my life."

EPILOGUE

"There is a very good reason why we fear the dark."
Willow Skin, the Wereding Chronicles.

Deep in the bowels of the earth, the vast shadow that was the Wraith King stared down from his high gallery. His glowing coal eyes watched as huge misshapen figures strove among massive fires, their muscles bulging as they filled the vast cavern with the pounding of metal on metal, forging masses of arms and armour. The scrape of a boot on stone reminded the shadow lord that he was not alone.

"Does the work please you, lord?" asked the raw, rasping voice of his orc companion.

"The quotas are being met, Grast," responded the Wraith King in his soul chilling voice that appeared to freeze the very air it passed through. "Whether the army will serve, remains to be seen."

"My brothers will not fail you," Grast said through the half healed wound that crossed his throat.

"They had better not, Grast, or you will have to face my wrath. Do not forget that I gave you back your life. I can take it away just as easily as I gave it to you."

That warning silenced Grast and for a long time the Wraith King could feel the orc's glare burning into his cloaked back. Not that the Wraith King cared about Grast's hate, but his presence was beginning to irritate him.

"Is there something else, Grast?"

"The Lord Tahane is waiting to speak to you."

"Here?"

"He is in the outer chamber."

"Then show him in."

The Wraith King did not turn when he heard the hissing voice behind him. He did not take his eyes off the hive below.

"I hope your army is ready to march."

"It soon will be," the Wraith King replied. "I see you return empty handed."

"There were complications," snarled the hooded figure of Tahane.

"So I have heard. It is surprising how great a complication a stripling girl can be."

"If you were scrying, you might have noticed there was more than just a stripling girl."

"However you put it, you failed to obtain the rod," snapped the Wraith King.

Tahane hissed like a angry cobra and cast back his dark hood to reveal the horned, skull face of the Fire Drake in miniature atop a man's body. Its long, forked tongue flickered out, its length flickering with tiny flames.

"Don't mock me, necromancer, you are not my master."

"No, but I do have orders from him for you."

"What would the Fire Lord have me do?"

"He would have you mirror in the south what is happening in the north."

"You are speaking in riddles, Wraith," Tahane snarled.

"This slip of a girl who troubled you has a sister. The Fire Lord would have you be her ally."

"Ah, so it is to be a deceitful game, is it?"

"You dragons do like your games."

"Wheels within wheels, Wraith," hissed the Fire Drake in human form.

"The Fire Lord orders you to befriend this girl and be her steed in the coming war."

"A steed," Tahane snarled.

"If your pride can stomach it, of course. I wonder which will give first, your pride or the battle?"

"Have a care, Wizard, remember that I tolerate you only because he orders me to."

"But he does order you, and whether you like it or not, you are his servant."

"For now," Tahane hissed softly.

"Dragon games," the Wraith King muttered. "Well, like it or not you must obey as I do, so leave me and go south. Leave me to my war. I will call you if I need you."

"One day, Wraith Lord, I will not come, or if I do come I will burn you where you stand."

"Perhaps, but until then go and do your master's bidding."

"I will, but remember that he is also your lord and one day he will order your destruction."

"Until then, Fire Drake, I say get you gone."

Tahane hissed with barely contained rage, and turning, he strode out of the cavern.

"Well, Fire Lord, your die is cast," whispered the Wraith King as he watched a spray of sparks from the anvils. "Soon, very soon, the chess pieces will go forth, but who will win, the black or the white, it will be interesting to see. Not that it matters, whoever wins will only increase my power and once I am done even the Fire Lord will serve me, and then I will rule the world. When I do I will make both these sisters my slaves."

Request from the author

If you have enjoyed reading *The Awakening of Magic*, please write a brief review on your bookseller's web page which features this book.

e.g.

https://www.amazon.co.uk/Awakening-Magic-Book-Wereding-Chronicles/dp/1782223835/

I'd really appreciate it.

Thanks,
Christian Boustead

About the author

Christian Boustead is a blind author who lives in Hanley, Staffordshire. This is the first novel he published, but it isn't his last...

If you wish to learn more about Christian and his works please visit his website:

https://findbooksinside.wordpress.com/2016/03/19/meetauthor-christian-boustead/

Extract from Dragon Games

Book Two of the Wereding Chronicles

"... When Robin opened the heavy cover of the book, it was to find it was a dictionary of the old tongue, the ancient language used in the mists of time and which was sometimes used by the noble houses to embellish their coats of arms. Robin knew a few words of this language, and she had been taught her own family motto by the late Scholar Galmor years ago, so many of the symbols and words before her felt familiar even if she could not actually recognise or interpret them. Her own motto, "Rosa ess Swarvace, bet Falcos fallow laz t'e dona balt," meaning, *The rose is sweet, but the eagle falls like a thunder bolt*, helped her to pick out the words that made up this motto, but other than that she found most of the rest of the words unfamiliar.

She glanced across at her two fellow students who sat on either side of her at identical desks, studying, from what Robin could make out, the same books as her own, although by the look of it they were both further along. Robin was about to turn her attention back to the book when Calador, who may have spotted her glance, decided to test her.

"Canduss, the words for the four elements?"

"Terra, Ventus, Insendium and aqua," Robin heard herself say, almost amazed that she knew the answer, but she did.

"It seems we have a prodigy." Calador sneered at her and Robin was not sure if he was pleased or angry. "Perhaps she can give me the words to the ignite spell."

Robin, of course, had no idea what the master was talking about, though she felt she could tell him given a little more time. She had been surprised she could tell him the names of the elements and realised that she suddenly understood many of the characters that had, until that moment, mystified her. It was as though a window in her mind opened and showed her some hidden key. The key was not revealed to Robin, but somehow it gave her the understanding to interpret the complicated symbols, and she knew what the word was and how she could take individual characters and make them words that were now clear in her minds-eye. It was as though the words were written in fire across her mind.

"Incendium..." Robin heard her own voice say, the words escaping her lips before she could stop them.

The effects of these words were remarkable. The tall man narrowed his eyes and staring coldly at her, turned away and left the room.

"We may all pay for that," Alfred whispered.

"I'm sorry! I didn't mean to say it," Robin whispered back.

"It doesn't matter, Robin," Cara said softly. "If you can read, you will soon please him."

"I don't want to please him," Robin spat. "I want to cast magic."

"You will, you will," soothed the other girl.

"But it was another two days before she was allowed to cast a spell. She had gone leaps and bounds with the old language and before very long Calador was speaking to her in the old tongue and Robin, who had grasped an almost magical skill with the language, answered him easily, as if she had been speaking it all her life. This meant that he was, by the third day, willing to let Robin practice a spell. She and her fellow students, were gathered into the central courtyard that formed a well round which the tower circled. This lesson took place at night and the moon, just past full, shone down on the small pool that sat at the centre of the paved yard. Robin felt a thrill anticipating the upcoming magic, although Calador had not told them what he would be teaching them. She wondered if it would be some kind of elemental spell, as he had talked about the manipulation of fire with an almost loving tone in his voice. That thought, however, made her frown as she stared down into the almost mirror calm waters. If he wanted to teach them about fire magic, wouldn't they have been better practicing that in one of the magically protected chambers that Cara and she had cleaned out once.

"Do you see anything in the water, Canduss," Calador's voice whispered in her ear, making Robin jump, for she had not heard him approach. "Do you intend to learn the lesson without me?"

Robin bit back a retort, and managing to control her anger and gather her courtesy, spoke in a voice devoid of a tremor. "Master Calador how can I learn a lesson without you, when I don't even know what the lesson is?"

Her only answer was one of his cold, enigmatic smiles that Robin found infuriating.

"What are we here to learn, master?" Alfred asked, switching his gaze from Calador to Robin and back again.

"We are here to learn how to scry," Calador said, standing on the opposite side of the pool from the three students.

"Scrying, what shall we see?"

"That depends, Alfred. What is your heart's desire? What would you wish to see? Who do you seek?"

Robin suddenly thought of Rose. This would be her way of finding her, but even as she thought this she was distracted as the desire to see Luna almost drove Rose from her head. Both their faces were driven from her mind as Caladors cold voice cut into her thoughts.

"Canduss, perhaps you would like to join us."

"I am sorry, master," Robin apologised and averted her eyes from his cold gaze.

"Concentrate," the master said. "I am about to teach you something important, so watch me carefully or you might miss a vital component."

Robin watched, as from a belt pouch the black master removed a small leather bag, from which he took a pinch of dried leaves.

"This is dried rosemary," he said, sprinkling it over the pool. "Now, remembering to summon the power from within you, visualise what you wish to see and speak the words of power, Speculum revelum."

As he said this, the mirror of the lake seemed to mist, as if a giant had breathed on a mirror. Then the mist cleared to reveal to them all an image of a high mountain pass, silvered by the moon. Then the image was gone and the pool was a blank silver disk.

"Very well, who wants to go next?"

Alfred accepted the bag of rosemary next and when he cast the spell an image of a young girl lying in a bed appeared, but the image only lasted a second before a single tear fell from Alfred's eyes to send ripples spreading across the image, distorting and then shattering it.

"Control," Calador snapped at the little boy. "You will never gain mastery, if you let your emotions rule you, boy."

Cara's scrying was misty and seemed to show a castle tower, but either it was surrounded by fog or for some reason the casting was not working.

"Did I do something wrong, master?"

"Uncertain," the master sighed. "Something maybe interfering with the scrying."

Cara did not respond to that, but passed the bag to Robin. Robin hated herself for doing it, but she thrust all thoughts of Luna from her and summoned Rose's face before her mind's eye and spoke the words. She watched as the water clouded and could not believe it when the mist cleared to show her sister lying in some grey room, was it a cell? Robin thought that Rose was dressed in strange leathers, but the image was not clear and as she watched a curtain of clouds rolled across it.

Robin felt the power coiling inside her as she commanded the magic to show her Rose. The cloud cleared, but the image that appeared suddenly was not her sister, but a large horned, reptilian head covered in bright red scales. Robin felt its glowing red orbs meet and lock with hers. She heard the beast roaring in her ears and then all was black.

***

Robin (Rose's sister), wishes to find her sister who disappeared after their father's killer, but she, too, is hunted by the wolf helmed Kain, who killed her father.

She must harness her magic before it turns her into a red skinned monster. At the same time she attempts to find what she can about the mysterious Weredings who may have kidnapped her sister.

Dragon Games, Book Two of the Wereding Chronicles

ISBN 978-1-78222-450-1

Lightning Source UK Ltd.
Milton Keynes UK
UKHW020658261119
354268UK00011B/1147/P